THE TOWN THAT WOULDN'T DIE
THE CROCKETTS' WESTERN SAGA: 4

ROBERT VAUGHAN

WOLFPACK
PUBLISHING
— EST 2013 —

WOLFPACK
PUBLISHING
— EST 2013 —

Published in the United States by Wolfpack Publishing, Las Vegas

Wolfpack Publishing
5130 S. Fort Apache Road, 215-380
Las Vegas, NV 89148

wolfpackpublishing.com

Paperback ISBN 978-1-64734-791-8
eBook ISBN 978-1-64734-790-1

THE TOWN THAT
WOULDN'T DIE

Chapter One

The afternoon tranquility was broken by two men riding at a gallop down the middle of Main Street. They whooped and shouted and fired their pistols in the air and the long-suffering citizens of Sulphur Springs could do nothing but shiver in fear and resignation. They pulled back even deeper into the homes and businesses where they were taking refuge.

From the second floor of Caswell's Hardware Store, Hugh Young, the barber, pulled the window shade to one side and looked down at the two riders.

"What is it?" someone asked. "What's going on?"

"Nothing, really. Just a couple of the sheriff's deputies having a little fun," Young answered, accenting the word fun. "It's Deputies Taylor and Cutter. They're just shooting into the air."

"Even just shooting into the air is dangerous enough,"

George Kidder said. "A couple of weeks ago I had to re-place a window in front of my feed store because one of the deputies got drunk and began shooting wildly."

"Be glad it was just a windowpane," one of the others said.

"Yes, you're right. What if my wife or one of my children had been in front of the store?"

"Seems to me like the very least we could expect is for a body to be safe in his own house or place of business," Cliff Caswell said.

"It's strange, isn't it that we are being terrorized by the very people who are supposed to protect us?" Clarence Watson asked. Watson was editor of the Valley Gazette, the town newspaper. "I'm telling you men, we've got to do something about it."

Young left the shade fall back in place, then returned to his chair to rejoin the others. This was an impromptu town meeting of most of the merchants and businessmen of the town. The meeting had been suggested by Clarence Watson as a way of discussing what they could do to ease the situation in a town that was being run in a roughshod fashion by a sheriff who had declared Sulphur Springs an "open town." Cliff Caswell had opened the front part of the upstairs of his hardware store for the meeting. The back half of the second floor of the hardware store was occupied by Doc Tanner's office. Doc Tanner was also present.

"Perhaps we should do nothing," Parson Neustadt suggested. Ostensibly Methodist, Parson Neustadt was aware of his position as the only Protestant minister in town, and thus accommodated an ecumenical congregation, even offering to dunk those who preferred an immersion type baptism. There was also a Roman Catholic church, over on Third Street, on the other side of the railroad tracks, but it's priest, Father Gomez, tended to a flock that was mostly Mexican, and neither the padre nor any of his parish were present for the meeting.

"What do you mean we could do nothing, Parson?" Walter Levy, the owner of the leather goods store, asked. "By God, we've tried doing nothing, and it hasn't worked. Excuse my language."

"No, we haven't done nothing," the parson said. "I mean, we haven't actively done nothing."

"Parson, what in the Sam Hill are you talking about?"

"Think about it for a moment, gentlemen. Why does anyone come to a town like this in the first place?" Parson Neustadt asked. "They come to town for the goods and services a town can provide: food, clothing, saddles, guns and ammunition, beer, whiskey, haircuts... everything that civilization offers. Now, suppose we didn't offer anything here? Suppose we got every merchant to shut down his business?"

"For how long?"

"For as long as it takes," the parson answered. "When the sheriff and his deputies can no longer take advantage of the things a town has to offer...when they can no longer collect a 'sheriff's tax' because no business is being done...why, perhaps they'll leave our town and go somewhere else."

"In other words, make Sheriff Greenwall be someone else's worry?" Caswell asked.

"Well, yes, in a manner of speaking," the parson admitted

"And what about the townspeople during that time?" John Watkins asked. Watkins was proprietor of the general store. "I've got folks who depend on me. What are they supposed to do for food and clothing?"

"Yeah, and what about the rest of us merchants?" Levy asked. "How are we supposed to make a living?"

"I didn't say it would be easy," Parson Neustadt replied. "I just said it was a possibility, something we might consider."

"Parson, I can't even begin to consider your recommendation," Doc Tanner said. "I've got a couple of women who are expecting children. Now, I know babies have been coming into this world long before there were doctors, but it looks like Mrs. Schlessinger is going to have a difficult birth. What if she starts to deliver? Am I supposed to just stand by and do nothing?"

"Well, no, of course not," the parson stammered. "I mean, I wouldn't expect you to just let someone die."

"Speaking of dying," Casper Verndam, the undertaker, put in, "suppose someone does die during this period. Am I to leave them unburied?"

"Well, no," the parson admitted

"And what about church on Sunday? Will you suspend it as well?"

"I wouldn't think so," the parson replied. "I mean, I would think that people would need God more than ever under such circumstances, wouldn't you?"

"All right, so how effective can we be, Parson?" Kidder asked. He began counting off the exceptions on his fingers. "Doc will be working, the undertaker will still be working, you'll still be working, and, like Watkins says, people will still need food. Besides that, the sheriff owns the Bon-Ton saloon, so you know it isn't going to be shut down. And Bertie Edgerton owns the Saddle Rock, but he's out of town right now, and you know Harry Connors won't shut it down without Edgerton telling him to. So where does that leave us?"

"That pretty much leaves us with no plan," Watson said

"Then, what are we going to do?" Young asked.

"What if we fight fire with fire?" Caswell suggested.

"What do you mean?"

"What if we could get someone to oppose Sheriff

Greenwall?"

"Oppose him? You mean run against him in an election?" Kidder asked.

"No, that wouldn't do any good," Caswell said. "Greenwall isn't going to let us have an election."

"Then, oppose him in what way?" Kidder asked.

"I mean did we find someone who will stand up to the sheriff and his deputies and do what it takes to clean up the town."

"Do what it takes?"

"Yes."

"You are just beating around the bush here, Caswell," Watson said. "Tell us exactly what you mean."

"I think he means kill the sheriff," Kidder said. He looked at Caswell. "That is what you mean, isn't it, Cliff?"

Caswell was silent for a moment, then he took a deep breath and let it out audibly. "Actually, I would prefer that Greenwall leave of his own accord if he is confronted. But if the only way we can get rid of him is to kill him, then, yes, that's what I mean," he finally said.

"Who do you propose to do that?" Kidder asked. "One of us?"

Caswell shook his head. "No," he said. "We aren't killers."

"Then who?"

"I don't know. Maybe we can find someone."

"You mean hire someone?"

"If necessary."

"To kill the sheriff? You are suggesting that we hire a killer?"

Caswell looked squarely at Kidder, then, without blinking an eye, said, "Yes. If we have to go out and hire a killer, then I think that is what we should do."

"God in heaven, listen to you men!" the parson gasped. "You are not only talking about murder; you are talking about doing it in such a way that the entire town will be involved."

"We are not talkin' about murder," Young said. "We're talkin' about standin' up for our rights."

"No, you aren't. You are talking about getting someone in here to commit murder. Gentlemen, I must tell you that a sin of that magnitude...the sin of murder... is not one that decreases as you increase the number of participants. Indeed, it is venal enough to corrupt all. If we do murder, gentlemen, it will make us no better than the men we are trying to eliminate," the parson said. "Can't you men see that?"

"Yeah, well, Preacher, sometimes there just isn't another way," Caswell said. "Not too many years back, you might recollect, this whole country was pushed into violence. We fought us one hell of a war, North and South. I was just a young man from Illinois then, but I picked up a gun and I went to war. And believe me, I saw enough killin' and dyin' at Antietam to last me a lifetime. But I didn't go through all that just so's I could come out west and kowtow to a bunch of varmints like Sheriff Greenwall and his deputies. No, sir, if somebody was to happen to kill that son of a bitch, as far as I'm concerned, he'd have my support."

Neustadt picked up his small, low-crown parson's hat and put it on his head.

"Gentlemen, I can't, in all good conscience, stay here while such a conversation is taking place. I will make no further effort to stop you, but neither can I actively support you. If you'll excuse me, I'll just be on my way."

"I'm real sorry you feel that way, Parson Neustadt," Caswell said. "I think that now, more than any other time, a town needs the moral guidance of a preacher."

"Moral guidance?" Parson Neustadt repeated. He sighed and shook his head. "God help me, I thought that was exactly what I was just trying to do for you. Good day, gentlemen."

The others watched Neustadt go down the stairs, then they heard the door down on the street open and shut.

"Ah, the hell with him. We don't need him anyway," Kidder said.

"Actually, we do. It would have been good to have him on our side. His support would have lent a degree of moral credence to what we are planning to do. It would have gone a long way toward getting' rid of any squeamishness some of the townspeople might have against killing the sheriff."

"Yes, well, no matter how you sugarcoat it, there's always going to be someone who'll call it by its name. The parson's right, it's murder, gentlemen. But, by God, I'm beginning to feel like it's the only thing left for us," Hammer said.

Across the street from the hardware store, the two deputies who had been discharging their weapons in the middle of the street a few minutes earlier were now inside the Bon-Ton saloon. Deputy Taylor, drinking whiskey from a bottle, walked over to look out across the top of the batwing doors onto the street. He turned the bottle up for a long, Adams-apple-bobbing drink, then he pulled the bottle down and wiped his mouth with the back of his hand.

"Hey, Cutter, come over here and look at this." Taylor said, laughing. "This is about the funniest lookin' thing I ever seen."

Cutter, who was also drinking his whiskey straight from the bottle, was leaning against the bar.

"What you see that's so funny Taylor?" he asked.

"The hat Parson Neustadt is wearing. Come over

here and take a gander at it."

Cutter walked over to the batwing doors. "What about it?" he asked.

"What about it? Hell, you blind? It's right there," Taylor said. "Look at the crown of that hat. Look how low down it is. Why, I bet it ain't no more'n two inches from the top of his head. And now, look how wide the brim is. Plus, it's got them two little black ribbons hangin' down the back. The fella that made that hat must've been drunk or somethin'."

Cutter took a drink of his whiskey then lowered the bottle. "Don't see nothin' all that funny about it. That's the kind of hat all preachers wear, far as I know."

"The hell you say?" Taylor examined the hat through eyes that seemed to be swimming in their sockets. "Bet I could shoot it off his head," he added.

"From how far?"

"From here."

Cutter measured the distance between the door of the saloon and the approaching preacher.

"The hell you say," he said. "That crown's pretty low, and he's a good hunnert and fifty feet away."

"It'd be a hell of a shot, I admit that. But I got me ten bucks says I can do it," Taylor insisted, taking out his pistol. "I'm just goin' to let him get a little closer."

"All right, I'll take that bet. But you see the other end

of that water trough?" Cutter pointed it out.

"Yeah, I see it. What about it?"

"That's too close. If you don't shoot the hat off before he gets there, the bets off."

"Get your ten bucks ready," Taylor said taking careful aim.

Back on the second floor of Caswell's Hardware store, George Kidder, feeling a need to stretch his legs, had gotten up and moved over to the window. He was watching the preacher walk down the street. Behind him he could hear the buzz of conversation as the businessman of the town continued to discuss the few options they had, with regard to how best they might handle the sheriff.

Suddenly Kidder saw a flash of light and a puff of smoke emerged from just inside the saloon door. A second later he heard the shot and at almost the same time he saw the preacher pitch backward. Neustadt fell on his back with his arms stretched out in the dirt on either side of him. His hat rolled off into the street, and his head was tilted back. Clearly visible, even from the second floor of the hardware store, was the large, bloody hole in the middle of Neustadt's forehead.

"Oh, my God!" Kidder gasped.

The others looked toward him.

"What is it, George? What'd you just see?"

"They just shot the preacher," Kidder said in a quiet, tight voice.

"What!" Young asked. He rushed over to the window, followed by the others.

"My God, who did it?"

"I don't know, exactly," Kidder said. "But I seen the puff of smoke. The shot come from the Bon-Ton."

Doc Tanner started quickly down the stairs.

"Doc, where you goin'?"

"To see if I can do anything for the preacher," the doctor called back over her shoulder

The others, galvanized into action by Doc Tanner's quick response, clomped rapidly and noisily down the stairs after him, then ran out into the street. By the time they reached Neustadt, there were already a couple of dozen people gathered around the preacher's prostrate form. The way Neustadt was lying, with his arms spread straight out to either side of him, reminded Kidder of Christ on the cross, though he didn't comment on it, for fear of someone taking affront for it being sacrilegious.

"Can you do anything for him, Doc?" Caswell asked.

Doc Tanner squatted down beside the body, then sighed and shook his head. "I'm afraid not. He was dead before he hit the ground," he said, standing up again. He looked around. "What the hell happened? Who shot him, and why?"

"I reckon I done it," Taylor said. He had been standing back with the others.

"You did it? You're a deputy. You're supposed to uphold the law," Doc said. "What possible reason could you have had?"

"Now, see here, Doc, I didn't do it of a pure purpose. It was a accident," Taylor said.

"An accident, you say? Would you mind telling me just how in the hell you can accidentally shoot someone right between the eyes?"

"I bet ten dollars with Deputy Cutter, here, that I could shoot that funny little hat off the preacher's head," Taylor said "I reckon I missed. I don't understand it, neither. I had me a real good bead on it. The preacher must of hopped up or something."

"You bet ten dollars?" Doc Tanner said angrily. "You took a man's life for ten dollars?"

"Take it easy, Doc," a new voice said. "You heard my deputy say it was a accident."

When Doc Tanner looked toward the new speaker, he saw Sheriff Sidney Greenwall just arriving on the scene.

"Deputy Taylor, that was mighty careless of you," Greenwall continued.

"Yeah," Taylor agreed, hanging his head contritely. "I'm real sorry 'bout that. Hell, I didn't have nothin' again' the preacher. For as I knew, he was a real nice fella."

"What are you goin' to do about it, Sheriff?" Kidder asked. "I mean you can't just treat this as if nothing has happened."

Greenwall exhaled audibly. "You're right. Taylor, Cutter, you're going to have to pay for this."

"Now, hold on here, Sheriff," Taylor said. "I done told you it was a accident. And I'm just real damn sorry for it. And I told these here folks how remorseful I am. Seems to me that ought to be the end of it."

"Yeah, well, bein' sorry ain't quite enough," Greenwall said. "What was that you said you bet? Ten dollars?"

"Yeah, ten dollars."

"All right, that would make the pot total twenty dollars. I'll take that twenty dollars."

"Wait a minute, Sheriff," Cutter said. "That ain't hardly right. The money's rightfully mine now. I won the bet. Besides which, I didn't shoot the son of a bitch, Taylor did. And the way you're doing it now, why, it's like Taylor ain't payin' a'tall, specially as how he already lost the money."

"You didn't shoot him but you... what's that word?" Greenwall asked. Then he smiled. "Oh, yeah, you aided and abetted. But you're right, Taylor needs to pay more, so I'll take twenty dollars from each of you."

"Wait a minute, that means I'm out a total of thirty dollars here," Taylor complained.

"Pay up," Greenwall ordered.

Grumbling, the two men handed over the money. "It don't seem right to me," Taylor said. "Hell, I told you it was an accident."

"Accident or not, the preacher's dead and he's goin' to need a decent buryin'," Greenwall said. He took the money from his two deputies then gave it to Verndam. "Undertaker, you see to it he gets buried good and proper," he said.

"I'm not chargin' nothing for the buryin'," Verndam said "I'll give this money to the preacher's church."

"I'm sure the preacher would like that," Greenwall said. "Come on, boys," he added, speaking to his deputies. "Let's get a drink and let these folks bury their preacher in peace."

"Caswell," Kidder said as Greenwall and his deputies walked back across the street toward the Bon-Ton. "You're right. Somebody's got to take care of that son of a bitch."

"I agree," Young said. "But who?"

"You know," Watson said, "I'm not really much of a religious man. But the preacher getting killed like that?" He shook his head. "I don't believe we're goin' to have to find anybody. I've got me a feeling that the Lord has already put things in motion to set things right again."

Chapter Two

On the evening of that same day, racing toward the brilliant scarlet and gold sunset beneath the darkening vaulted sky, the Southwest Flyer thundered across the mesquite-dotted landscape. Inside the Baldwin 4-4-0 locomotive, the engineer held the throttle wide open while his fireman threw chunks of wood into the roaring flames of the firebox. The train was exactly on schedule, whipping past a milepost every one hundred and twenty seconds.

Behind the engine and the tender was a string of coach cars, and, inside these, the travelers were getting down to the business of eating their supper. As there was no dining car, the passenger cars were filled with the smells of dried beef, hot peppers, spicy sausages, and smoked cheeses from the boxed lunches the passengers had brought on board with them.

Will Crockett was sitting in the last seat on the left side of the car. His legs were pulled up so that his knees rested on the seat back in front of him, and his hat was tilted down over his eyes. Unlike the others, he had no boxed lunch. He had eaten a piece of jerky at about three in the afternoon, and that would have to do, for now.

Will was going to Sulphur Springs, Arizona, where he would meet his brother Gid. During the late war Will and Gid had ridden with Quantrill and Bloody Bill Anderson. They were called Bushwhackers then, and though the name was meant to be derogatory; it was an appellation they now accepted with pride. The only survivors of their family, the two brothers generally ran together. But three weeks ago, Gid had accepted a job taking some horses to a ranch in West Texas. At the time, Will happened to be riding a winning streak in one of the local saloons, so he opted to stay on for a while.

Then, yesterday, a man named Bertie Edgerton drew a full house of aces and kings. To cover his bet he put forth a deed for the Saddle Rock, an establishment he claimed was the finest saloon in Sulphur Springs.

Will was holding three queens, and when he drew the fourth, Edgerton sighed, then pushed the deed across the table.

"You won it, Crockett, fair and square," he said.

"Would you like to buy it back?" Will asked. "I won't

hold you up."

Edgerton paused for a moment. "No," he said. "No, I don't think I do want to buy it back. It's a good saloon, Mr. Crockett, and there are some good people working there. They deserve something better than the best I can do for 'em. You may be the best thing that ever happened to them and the town."

Owning a saloon had never been in Will's plans, but now that he had drawn the hand, he decided he would play the cards. He sent a telegram to Gid suggesting that instead of coming back here, they should meet in Sulphur Springs. That was where he was headed now.

As he sat in his seat, rocked by the gentle rhythm of the train, he gradually slipped off to sleep. He had been sleeping for about an hour when the train suddenly ground to a shuddering, screeching, banging halt.

Will woke with a start.

"What is it?" someone asked.

"I don't know. The train is stopping for some reason," another answered.

"Well, if we're going to stop at every rock and cactus in the entire Southwest, the management of this railroad will certainly hear from me," the first man said. "This is no way to run a business."

Will looked through the window. It was very dark outside, but he did see several horses, shadows moving through the blackness. He knew instantly what was going on, so he pulled his pistol from his holster and let it rest on his knee, covering it with his hat.

Suddenly someone burst into the car from the front. He was wearing a bandanna tied across the bottom half of his face. He was holding a pistol, which he waved toward the passengers in the car.

"Everyone stay in their seats!" the masked man shouted.

"See here! What is the meaning of this? What is going on?" a man shouted indignantly. "I have already stated my intention of reporting this to the railroad, and this unseemly behavior will come in for special attention!"

He started to get up from his seat, but the gunmen moved quickly toward him and brought his pistol down sharply over the man's head. The passenger groaned and fell back. The woman who was with him cried out in alarm.

"Report to the railroad? You damned fool, we're robbin' this here railroad!" the gunman said gruffly. "Now, ever'one stay in their seats like I said! The next man that stands up, I aim to shoot."

Another gunmen came into the car to join the first.

"Any trouble in here?" he asked.

"Nothin' I can't handle myself. What's goin' on outside?"

"Ever'thing is goin' like it's supposed to, Danny. Gus is coverin' the engineer, and Raster is robbin' the mail car."

"Damn you, Deke! What the hell's the purpose for wearin' these masks, if you're goin' to call ever'one by name?"

"You're right. I wasn't thinkin'," Deke said.

"That's 'cause you got no brains to think with. Now, get on back to the next car and keep ever'one in their seats."

"How will I know when the rest of you leave?"

"Just keep your eyes open, that's all. Now, get on back there."

As the second gunman started down the aisle toward the next car, he looked over toward Will, then stopped.

"Mister, I don't like the way you're lookin' at me," the gunman said

"Let it be, friend," Will said. "Just go on about your business."

"Haw!" The gunman laughed out loud. He turned toward the other robber. "Hey, Danny, d' you hear what this fella said? He tol' me to jus' go on about my business."

"Will you shut your mouth, you damned fool," Danny said.

Flustered because he had fouled up again, the gunman turned back to Will.

"I don't like you, mister. How 'bout you just empty your pockets?"

"I told you to let it be," Will warned.

"Let it be? I'll show you how to let it be," the gunman

said. Swinging his pistol toward Will, he thumbed back the hammer, but that was as far as he got. Will pulled the trigger on his own gun, and a finger of fire stabbed through his hat. His slug caught the would-be robber in the chest, and the robber, shocked by the sudden turn of events, dropped his own gun then put his hand over his wound, trying to stem the quick flow of blood.

"What the hell?" Danny shouted from the front of the car. He fired and his bullet crashed through the glass beside Will, cutting his face with sharp shards of glass. The others in the car screamed and got down as Will returned fire. Danny staggered back, his hands to his throat, blood spilling through his fingers.

As the car filled with the gun smoke of the three discharges, Will got out of his seat and scooted out through the back door of the car. He jumped from the steps down to the ground, then fell and rolled off into the darkness.

"Danny, Deke! What's goin' on in there?" someone called. "What's goin' on?"

In the dim light that spilled through the car windows, Will saw the gunman who was yelling at the others. This was Gus, who had been covering the engineer, and now he was moving quickly toward the back of the train. As he ran through the little golden patches of light it had the effect of a lantern show, blinking on and off so that first he was in shadow, then illuminated, then in shadow, then illuminated.

Will raised his pistol and pointed toward the next window, waiting for Gus to pass through the light. But Gus had suddenly realized what he was doing, and he remained in the shadow.

"Gus!" a voice called from the darkness "Gus, we got to get!"

"Somethin's happened to Danny and Deke!" Gus called back.

"That's their problem! We got to get!"

"Danny's my brother!" Gus shouted. "I ain't leavin' my brother!"

"Have it your own way," the voice called from the darkness. "I'm gettin' out!"

Will heard horse's hooves as a rider hurried off into the darkness.

"Raster! Raster, you come back here, you son of a bitch!"

Gus began firing in the darkness, his bullets flying toward the galloping horse. Each time he fired, the two-foot wide flame pattern lit him up as brightly as a photographer's flash powder.

"Drop your gun, Gus," Will said "I've got a bead on you."

Gus suddenly spun and started firing toward the sound of Will's voice. He was firing blindly, but his bullets were coming frighteningly close, because Will could hear them whistling by.

Will returned fire, and Gus let out a little yell, then fell.

Will moved through the darkness toward them, then knelt alongside.

"Why didn't you leave when you had the chance?" he asked.

"You got a brother, mister?" Gus asked in a pained gasp.

"Yes."

"Then you ought not to have to ask that question. Me 'n Danny is all that's left. I couldn't leave him." He gasped a few more times, then his labored breathing stopped.

"You didn't leave him," Will said, straightening up and putting his gun away.

By now, with the shooting over, a few other brave souls were beginning to climb down from the train. Gradually they filled the space alongside the track, looking cautiously out into the darkness as they moved toward Will and the body that lay on the ground beside him.

"Is he dead?" one of the passengers asked.

"Yes," Will said.

"So's them two inside."

The engineer and the conductor appeared from the darkness.

"They get anything off any of the passengers?" the conductor asks.

"Not a penny, thanks to this man," someone said,

nodding toward Will.

"You should've seen him!" another said. "He took on all three of 'em, all by hisself."

"Mister, you're a genuine hero," the conductor said. "It's just too bad you weren't ridin' in the mail car."

"They get any money from there?" a passenger asked.

"I'll say they did. They got twelve hundred dollars," the conductor replied.

Someone whistled softly. "That's a good day's work."

"Yeah, especially when you figure it's all for one man," the engineer said.

"What do you mean, for one man?"

"Well, they was four of 'em stopped the train," the engineer said. "But when it was all over with, only one of 'em got away. He had the money and he's got no one to share it with."

'What are you goin' to do with the bodies?" one of the passengers asked.

"I don't know. I haven't really thought about it," the conductor replied.

"You can't leave 'em here."

"There's two dead in our car," another said. "Don't think I like that either."

"Get 'em into the baggage car," the conductor suggested. "We'll take 'em into Sulphur Springs and give 'em to the sheriff."

The town of Sulphur Springs had begun as a mining community. For more than two years, the Associated Mining Company of Sulphur Springs took out as much silver from their digs as was being mined at any other place in the country. During this time, several enterprising citizens discovered that there was more than one way to mine silver. Some did it with a pick and shovel, others did it with cards, or liquor, or a pretty smile and a shapely pair of legs.

Then, most of the veins played out, and the amount of silver being mined dropped dramatically. Concurrent with the depletion of the silver, however, was a major discovery of copper.

Not everyone was upset with the playing out of the silver mines. Silver, like gold, attracted get-rich-quick people. Copper, on the other hand, tended to attract only the most assiduous miners...the mining engineers and the hard-working men who labored in the open pits. These were the steady, sober-minded men who tended to start families and build towns. Such industriousness attracted stores, banks, schools, and freight and stage lines. There were also a few ranches nearby to take advantage of the railroad that came into town, and it began to look as if Sulphur Springs would become a real, productive city, until a man named Sidney Greenwall came into the picture.

Greenwall was a small, unattractive man, with a pock-marked face, a drooping black mustache, a hawk like nose, and narrow, obsidian eyes. It was, perhaps, that unattractiveness which made him an outcast from society. As a result, he had developed absolutely no social skills. He did, however, have one skill which marked him as a man with whom others would have to reckon. Sidney Greenwall was a gunman with so few moral compunctions about killing that he could take the life of another man as easily as he could step on a cockroach.

Greenwall came to Sulphur Springs when the mines were still producing silver. He had been hired by the mining company to provide security for the silver shipments. Some, who knew of Greenwall's spotted past—he had robbed a few banks and held up a stage or two—suggested that using him to guard the silver was like setting the fox to watch the hen coop. Others insisted that you must "set a thief to catch a thief" and saw no problems whatever with using Greenwall to guard the silver shipments.

After the silver played out, however, there was no longer a need to provide guards over the ore shipments. That was because it took so much copper to turn a profit that the freight wagon gave way to the railroad as the prime carrier. Thus, by the time Associated Mining completed its changeover from silver to copper, Greenwall and his men found themselves out of work.

But those who breathed a sigh of relief over that fact soon learned, to their dismay, that Greenwall had no intention of leaving Sulphur Springs. Instead, he bullied a few of the town's officials into appointing him as the town sheriff, and his men as deputies. Now, with badges on their vests, they moved along the boardwalks, or through the streets of the town, pushing any and all out of their way. They would sometimes go so far as to pistol-whip some poor soul who was too slow in avoiding them. There had even been a few killings, usually over a dispute in a card game, but always justified as "self-defense," or "killed while resisting arrest for card cheating." The climactic event had occurred earlier this same day, when two of Greenwall's deputies killed the preacher "accidentally" while acting upon a bet.

By now the situation had reached the point to where very few of the decent citizens of Sulphur Springs would dare venture out of their homes. That hurt the business of the town's merchants, and as the legitimate stores began closing, the town began dying.

Even as the town was dying, however, it flared brightly, as drinking, gambling, and whoring became its major industry. News of the "wide-open" town spread throughout the West so that it began to attract new residents. The new residents, however, were not the kind of people the original citizens of the town wanted, for they were nothing more than carbon copies of Greenwall and his men. As more hoodlums arrived, the number of those who were sucking out the life's blood of the town became disproportionate to the number of those whose industriousness supplied the life's blood of the town. And, like an animal being drained by leeches, the town was slowly, but inexorably, sinking to its knees.

Chapter Three

Will knew nothing of the killing of the preacher, or the town's history when, just after ten P.M., he stepped down onto the station platform in Sulphur Springs, Arizona. Behind him the train, while still, wasn't quiet. As it would be proceeding farther west, the firemen kept up the steam, and the relief valve continued to open and close in great, heaving sighs. Overheated wheel bearings and gearboxes popped and snapped as the tortured metal cooled. From the platform around him there came a discordant course of squeals, laughter, shouts, and animated conversations as people were getting on and off the train.

Looking toward the baggage car, Will saw that the train robbers had been taken from the train and laid out, side-by-side. Already, a crowd was gathering around the bodies.

Will found their morbid curiosity somewhat unsettling. There had been more than one train robbery in his own checkered past, and he knew there might be more in the future. He could well imagine his brother Gid and himself in the same situation as these three men.

One of the curious train passengers reach down to untie the kerchief from the neck of one of the dead outlaws.

"Hold on there, mister! Just what do you think you're a doin'?" someone asked.

"Takin' this here fella's kerchief," the curious passenger answered. "I aim to have me a souvenir."

"Leave it alone."

"Who the hell says so?"

"I say so," an authoritative voice replied. "I am Sheriff Sidney Greenwall, and if you try and take that kerchief, or anything else off any of these men, I'll throw you in jail."

Will looked toward Greenwall and saw a pock-faced man with the drooping mustache coming down the platform. Although he was a small man, there was the look of danger about him, and as he moved toward the bodies the assembled crowd parted before him, like the sea opening before Moses.

Greenwall wore his gun low on the right side. A five-pointed star, pinned to a leather vest, glinted in the light of the several flickering torches which illuminated the station platform.

"Sure thing, Sheriff," the passenger said. "Whatever you say."

"There's only three of 'em?" Greenwall asked. "Where's the other one?"

"There's only three killed," the conductor said. "There was another, but he got away...with the money shipment," he added.

"You don't say?" The sheriff stroked his chin. "And how much money would that be?" he asked.

"About twelve hundred dollars," the conductor answered. "It was a species transfer to the local bank."

A photographer hurried up to join them, lugging his camera and equipment. He set up the tripod, then started arranging the bodies, folding their arms across their chests. As an added touch, he put guns in their hands.

For a moment, Will had a touch of déjà vu, then he remembered that, during the late war, his lieutenant, Bloody Bill Anderson, had been photographed in the same gruesome way, right after he was killed.

"You ought to get a picture of that fella over there," someone said, pointing out Will. "He's the one kilt these outlaws."

"You don't say? All by hisself?" the photographer asked.

"Yep."

Smiling obsequiously, the photographer started toward Will.

"Mister, perhaps you'd like your picture taken with them boys?" he suggested. "I could make you a nice

35

copy for, oh, a dollar."

"And then sell copies of them to the public?" Will replied. "No thanks."

"Just tryin' to be helpful is all," the photographer said. "Most folks would want recognition for what they done."

The sheriff looked toward Will. "That right, mister? You the one shot these three men?"

"I'm the one."

"What's your name?"

"Crockett."

"Don't reckon I've ever heard of you," Greenwall said.

"Just as well," Will replied. "It's not a good sign when sheriffs start learning a man's name before he ever comes to town." He tried to make a joke, but the sheriff was a humorless man.

"How is it that you shot these three, while you let the one with the money getaway?"

"Wasn't my job to protect the bank's money, Sheriff," Will answered. He nodded toward the bodies. "Wasn't even my job to stop these fellas, and if they hadn't shot at me first, I wouldn't of shot them."

A sudden lightning flash of magnesium powder indicated that the photographer had started his work.

"You sayin' they shot first, but you still bested 'em?" the sheriff asked, the expression on his face and the tone of his voice suggesting that he didn't quite believe Will.

"That's what I'm sayin'," Will replied.

"Yes. Well, it is curious, though, don't you think?" the sheriff asked. "I mean, if you and the fella who got away had worked out some sort of deal, why, you'd both be settin' pretty now, wouldn't you? With only the two of you to share in the money."

"Greenwall, you accusing me of being in on this?" Will asked.

"No," Greenwall said. "Not exactly. But I am the sheriff here, and I am supposed to think on such things. It's my job."

"You think on it all you want," Will said. "But don't be makin' any accusations you can't back up."

"Ain't makin' none," the sheriff said. "But if I was, believe me, I could back them up. Just thought I'd let you know, though, that I aim to keep my eye on you for as long as you're in town."

Along either side of the street leading into town, false-fronted shanties competed for space. Subdued bubbles of soft light shone from the windows of the houses, while the saloons spilled a much brighter, golden light onto the boardwalks. The street was noisy with the cacophony of saloon patrons having a good time. From the nearest saloon came a man's hoarse guffaw, followed by a woman's high-pitched cackle. Someone broke a glass, and the crashing, tinkling sound enjoyed a moment of supremacy.

There were two saloons in town and Will looked at both of them. One of them had a gilt-painted sign, reading: THE BON-TON. He also saw that saloon was the center of all the noise and laughter, as it was doing a booming business.

The other saloon had no sign, and very little business. By the process of elimination, he decided that this was the Saddle Rock. Since this was the saloon he had won in a poker game, this was the one he headed for.

He pushed in through the batwing doors. To the left, as he entered, was a long bar. Towels hung on hooks about every five feet along its front. Behind the bar, a large mirror stretched the length of the wall. The paucity of customers in the place was reflected by the many empty tables Will saw in the mirror.

As he looked around, Will was somewhat surprised by the lack of patrons, because with all the oak, glass, and gilt, this was obviously a very decent place. Why, then, was the Bon-Ton bursting at the seams with customers, while this place was practically empty? The question was much more than the mere curiosity of a customer. As he was the new owner, that was information he felt entitled to know. For the time being, however, he decided to keep to himself the fact that he was the new owner.

Will stepped up to the bar, and the bartender slid down toward him.

"We got whiskey and beer," the bartender said. "Which will it be?"

"What kind of whiskey?"

"Old Overholt. Two dollars the bottle, or ten cents the shot. Beer's five cents a glass."

"I'll have a beer."

The bartender pulled a glass down from a shelf in front of the mirror, then put it under the spigot and pulled the handle. Golden liquid slid up the inside of the glass then stopped at the top, where it was crowned by a foaming head.

"Thanks," Will said, taking the beer. He blew some of the foam off, then took a drink. The beer was good, so that couldn't be the cause of the lack of customers. Turning his back to the bar, he looked out over the saloon at the few who were patronizing the Saddle Rock.

At the far end of the bar a young woman was drinking a beer. Her reddish-brown hair radiated in a wild array around her face, then cascaded down her back and across her shoulders. The dress she wore showed a generous amount of cleavage, and for a moment Will enjoyed the luxury of letting his eyes wander across her full breasts, flat, slender belly, and gently swelling hips. Smiling, he lifted his beer toward her. Lifting her own beer, she returned the smile.

"Would you care to have a drink with me, miss?" Will asked

"Yes, I'd be glad to. Thank you," the woman replied, smiling as she moved down the bar to join him.

"One for the lady, barkeep."

"My name is Phoebe," the lady said. "And you are?"

"Crockett. Will Crockett."

The bartender put a drink in front of Phoebe, then slid a coin across the bar to Will.

"Your change, mister."

"Wait a minute," he said. "You're a little light, aren't you?"

"No, that's right."

"I believe you said beer was five cents?"

"That's right."

"I gave you a quarter, I bought two beers. I should get fifteen cents back. There's only a nickel here."

"A nickel each for the beers, and another nickel each for the sheriff's tax."

"The sheriff's tax? What the hell is the sheriff's tax?"

"If you want my opinion, it's not a tax at all. It's downright stealin'," the bartender said.

"Harry, if I were you, I'd be careful about sharing my opinions," someone said. "You never know who's listening." The speaker, also standing at the bar, was an older, gray-haired man. He was rather well-dressed in a brown suit.

The bartender chuckled. "Now, that's real funny, hearin' such a thing from you, Doc, seein' as how you've never been known to shy away from sharin' your opinions with anyone."

"Well, that's different," Doc replied. "I'm an old man. Old people can get away with more things than young people can. Besides, I'm the only medical doctor within fifty miles, and the kind of town Greenwall runs generates a rather high demand for a doctor. He can't afford to lose me. On the other hand, bartenders are a dime a dozen. You, my friend, can be replaced in a heartbeat." The gray-haired man looked at Will, then stuck out his hand. "Jason Tanner is the name, sir. But, as Harry said, I am a doctor, so most folks just call me Doc."

At that moment, a new patron pushed through the batwing doors and stepped into the saloon. Seeing Will, he stepped up to the bar.

"Say, you're the one that killed them outlaws, ain't you?" he asked.

"Yes," Will answered without elaboration.

"What outlaws?" Phoebe asked.

"Some outlaws tried to hold up the train tonight," the customer said. He pointed to Will. "This here fella killed three of 'em and drove the fourth one off."

"You took on three men, all by yourself?" Phoebe asked, obviously impressed with the idea.

"Not willingly," Will replied. "What actually happened was they took me on. I didn't have much choice but to fight back."

"And kill all three of 'em," the recently arrived patron said. He chuckled. "I gotta tell you, mister, you've sure set the town to talkin'. Even Greenwall was impressed by what you done."

"You must be pretty good with a gun," Harry suggested. "Are you? Or were you just lucky?"

"A little of both, I guess," Will said modestly. "I was in the war. Folks get real familiar with guns during wartime."

"That's a fact, mister, it truly is," Harry replied. "I was in the war myself. Fifth Texas Artillery, it was. Who were you with?"

"I was with Quantrill," Will answered.

Harry's eyes grew big. "With Quantrill, you say? Everybody's heard of him. It was a pretty nasty bunch of boys that rode with him."

There was a time in Will's life when he would've taken offense at Harry's remark. But it was an accurate remark, innocently stated, so Will just chuckled. "Well, we weren't Sunday School boys," he admitted.

"You goin' to be stayin' in town?" Harry asked.

"Yes, I figure on staying around for a while," Will replied.

"You plannin' on becoming one of Greenwall's deputies?" Doc asked.

Will snorted what could've been a laugh. "Now, why would I want to do something like becoming a deputy?"

"Don't get me wrong. I'm certainly not recruiting for the sheriff," Doc replied. "But the truth is, being one of Greenwall's deputies is about the best job you can get in Sulphur Springs."

"Is that a fact? I never knew that deputies were so well paid," Will replied.

"I reckon they're not in most places," Harry said. "But Greenwall runs things a little different. He pays his deputies out of the tax he collects. And since he collects a lot of tax, he pays 'em well."

"And that's not all," Doc added. "In addition to the taxes Greenwall and his men collect, they also enjoy special reduced rates for the goods they buy from any of the merchants. Hell, they practically steal anything they want, and there's nothing we can do about it. We can't go to the law; they are the law!"

"They are bullies, all of them," Phoebe said bitterly. "They walked down the sidewalks, or through the streets of the town, just pushing people aside as if they own the entire town."

"And the killings," Harry said. "Don't forget the killings."

"Yes," Doc put in. "There have been several killings, though they are always found innocent by reason of self-defense."

"Or like the killin' today," Harry said. He told about the preacher getting killed as a result of a bet between two drunk deputies as to whether or not one of them could shoot the hat off the preacher's head. "That one was ruled an accident."

"You mean Greenwall has the judge bullied as well?" Will asked.

Doc laughed bitterly. "Hell, Mr. Crockett, Greenwall is the judge," he said.

"Now, do you see how being a deputy can pay so well?" Harry asked.

"I see what you're saying," Will said. "But I have no intention of working for him." He looked at Phoebe, smiling broadly. "The fact is, I'm going to work here, in the saloon."

"You're going to do what?" Phoebe asked, surprised by his statement. "Doing what?"

"Doing whatever I need to," Will answered. He still had not told them he was the new owner.

"Mr. Crockett, the fella that owns the place is out of town right now," Harry said, "and I can't speak for him.

But even if he was here, I don't think he would hire you. It's not that he wouldn't want to, or even that you wouldn't be a good man to have around here. But he can't afford it. Hell, he's way behind in payin' me my wages. This place just isn't making any money."

Will looked around the saloon. "I noticed that there aren't many customers. Why is that? This seems like a decent enough place to me. You'd think a place like this would make lots of money."

"It used to make lots of money," Harry answered. "Why, there wasn't a saloon between here and Tucson that done any better. But ever since the sheriff slapped on his tax, business has been way down."

"The saloon down the street seems to be doing all right," Will observed.

"I'll say it is," Harry replied. "We used to have two other bartenders in here, but they went down the street to work. Same thing with all the girls. Phoebe's the only one who stayed."

"And you stayed," Will said to Harry.

"Yes," Harry answered. "I might be crazy, but I stayed."

"Why?" Will asked. "I mean if you're making no money. Why did you stay?"

Harry continued to wipe glasses as he glanced around the saloon. "Bar keeping isn't just a job for me," he said. "It's a profession. And a fella ought to practice his profession in a place he can be proud of. I couldn't work in the Bon-Ton. I don't want to work in a place where they water their whiskey and they cheat their customers."

"I feel the same way," Phoebe said. "I might be a soiled dove, but I do have some honor."

Will looked at Phoebe, then smiled. "Well, I don't know about the girls who left here to go over there," he said, "but without even looking, I believe I'd have to say that the Saddle Rock got the best end of the bargain."

Phoebe returned his smile. "Why, thank you, sir," she said. "What a nice thing to say."

"It does make me curious, though," Will continued. "Why is the Bon-Ton doing so much better than the Saddle Rock?"

"That's an easy enough question to answer," Harry said. "Folks who buy a drink in here have to pay the sheriff's tax. Folks who buy a drink at the Bon-Ton don't. That means they can drink twice as much, for the same amount of money."

"The Bon-Ton doesn't pay any taxes? Why is that?"

"Because Sidney Greenwall owns it," Harry answered.

Chapter Four

Gid's coffeepot was suspended over the open flames, and the handle was so hot that he had to use his hat in order to pour himself a second cup of coffee. He was about to hang the pot up again when he sensed, rather than saw or heard, that someone was watching him. The hair on the back of his neck stood on end, and he forced himself to take a slow, deep breath, in order to remain calm.

"I got me almost a whole pot of good coffee here if you're in the mind for some," he said easily.

There was a quiet chuckle from the dark, then Gid heard the sound of someone walking. A moment later a man appeared in the edge of the golden bubble of light cast from the small campfire.

"I guess I wasn't as quiet as I thought I was," the man said. He took a collapsible cup from his pocket and held it out. "Don't mind if I do," he added.

Gid poured the coffee and examined the man closely. The stranger had clear, blue eyes, a long, narrow face, and a bushy beard. Gid had never seen him before.

"That's kind of dangerous, isn't it?" Gid asked. "I mean, comin' up on a man's camp as quiet as all that."

The stranger took the cup, then squatted on his heels. He slurped a swallow of coffee through lips extended slightly to allow the coffee a chance to cool.

"I don't know, you might be right," the stranger admitted. "The truth is, I've never been able to figure out which way is best. Some folks are so nervous they'll just start banging away the moment they hear you, without even giving you a chance to explain yourself. People like that, it's generally best for them to never even know you're in the area."

"Yeah," Gid said, still eyeing the stranger suspiciously. "But I'm not like that."

"No, I reckon you ain't," the stranger said. He chuckled again, but this time, in the middle of his laugh, he winced in pain, and he put his hand to his side.

"You all right?"

"Yeah, I'm fine. My horse threw me, that's all."

"You don't look like a man who'd be easily thrown," Gid suggested.

"Yeah, well, sometimes things happen."

Gid continued to keep a wary eye on the man. That

was when he saw blood on his side.

"You're bleeding," he said. "How'd you wind up bleeding from getting thrown?"

"Well, it's this way," the man said. He pulled his jacket back as if to show his wound. Then, suddenly, a gun appeared in his hand. "I wasn't exactly throw'd," he said. "I was shot."

Gid cursed himself for his stupidity. He was suspicious of the man from the very beginning and had been keeping a close eye on him; still, the man managed, somehow, to get the drop on him.

"Who shot you?"

"I ain't exactly sure who it was," the stranger admitted. "One minute me and three of my pards was holdin' up this train, and the next minute all hell was breakin' loose. Some passenger come offen the train with his gun blazin'. I think he kilt my three pards, an' somebody hit me an' my horse as we was ridin' away. Kilt my horse too. Left him lying about two miles back in the dark."

"Sounds to me like you and your pards would've been better off back in some town, drinkin' beer and sportin' the pretty girls," Gid said

"Yeah, well, my pards, may be," the stranger admitted. "They're lying back there as dead as my horse. But me, I got away." He patted his pockets. "And I got me over a thousand dollars of the railroad's money," he added. "With no one I have to share it with."

"With a bullet in your side and a dead horse, you aren't in that good of a shape," Gid suggested.

"Half hour or so ago, I woulda agreed with you," the stranger said. "But then I seen your fire, and I figured my luck had changed. Looks like I'm going to be needin' your horse."

Gid shook his head. "Sorry," he said. "My horse isn't for sale."

"Don't need no bill of sale, mister. Just your horse. I plan on leavin' your carcass here. You got five seconds to make your peace."

"Don't need to make my peace," Gid said. "All I need is to finish my coffee."

"Go ahead," the stranger said generously. "No need of me sendin' a man to hell on an empty stomach."

"Mind if I warm it?" Gid asked, reaching for the pot with his left hand.

"Go ahead. Just don't get any fancy ideas about tossin' the coffee in my face. If I see that pot so much as wiggle, I'm shootin'."

"Yeah, well, you're going to shoot me anyway, aren't you?" Gid replied. He began pouring coffee with his left hand and poured too much so that it splashed down over the edge of the cup, running onto his hand.

"Damn, that's hot!" he shouted in pain, dropping

the cup.

The stranger laughed. "Yeah, well, it ain't goin' to hurt too long, 'cause—"

That was as far as he got, for as Gid dropped his cup, his hand also dipped to the pistol at his side. He pulled it and fired before the stranger caught on to what he was doing. The bullet caught the stranger in the center of his chest, knocking him down before he could react by pulling the trigger of his own pistol.

Gid cocked his pistol for a second shot, but he saw immediately that a second shot wouldn't be needed.

"Damn!" the stranger said with an expulsion of breath. "Damn, damn, you got me good with that one. Where'd you learn a trick like that?"

"I don't know," Gid said. "It just came to me, I guess." He eased the hammer down on his pistol, then knelt beside the wounded man. He could see the blood frothing at the entry hole, and he knew his bullet had penetrated the lungs. He tore off a piece of the man's shirt and stuck it in the hole to slow the bleeding, but he knew he was just wasting his time.

"No use in doin' all that," the wounded man said, indicating that he too knew it was a waste of time. "I can hear this wound suckin' air. Ain't never know'd anybody to survive a wound like that. Have you?"

"No," Gid replied.

The stranger tried to chuckle, but the attempt turned into a hacking cough. "Hell," he said. "You coulda lied to me... tried to make me feel better."

"Why would I want to do that? Weren't you planning on killing me?"

"I reckon I was, at that. Tell you what you do. You take this here money I stole...sure as hell ain't goin' to do me no good now... an' you ride on into Sulphur Springs and have yourself a good time. My name's Raster. Pete Raster. There is a girl in Sulphur Springs, works at the Bon-Ton."

Raster interrupted his talk with a coughing spasm that sprayed blood onto his beard and shirt. Finally, he was able to talk again.

She calls herself Lily Bird, but her real name is Lucy Raster. She's my sister. I'd like you to tell her you run across me as I was dyin'. No need to tell her how I died, or that you was the one that kilt me. But I'd like her to know what happened to me."

"I'll do that," Gid promised. "Anything else I can do that'll—" He stopped in mid-sentence when he saw that Raster had quit breathing.

It was nearly midnight when Gid reached Sulphur Springs. The hoofbeats of his horse clomped hollowly as he rode into the dark town. Golden bubbles of light were splashed out onto the street, and Gid passed through them, in and out of light and shadow so that his face was now glowing, now dark.

The fact that the outlaw, Pete Raster, wanted him to come to Sulphur Springs was a coincidence. In fact, Gid was going to Sulphur Springs anyway, in response to a telegram from his brother.

MEET ME IN SULPHUR SPRINGS, the telegram had read in a frugal use of words, giving no explanation as to why he wanted him there, or where they would meet.

The why of it didn't matter much to Gid. If his brother wanted to meet here in Sulphur Springs, that was good enough for him. And as for the where...well, what better place to meet than a saloon? Besides which, he might be able to locate Raster's sister and kill two birds with one stone.

Gid guided his horse toward the brightest and loudest building in town. It seemed another fortuitous coincidence to Gid that this was the Bon-Ton.

Inside, the saloon was lighted by one huge, bright chandelier, as well as by a dozen or so kerosene lanterns. The bar was crowded, and the tables were full. At least half a dozen of the men were wearing deputy's badges, and Gid hesitated for a moment before he went any farther. Although he didn't believe there was any paper out on him or his brother at the moment, there had been plenty of paper in the past during their time with Quantrill, and immediately after the war. Therefore, being in the midst of so many lawmen was not necessarily his idea of a good time.

He noticed, however, that the others, those who were not wearing badges, seemed totally unintimidated by those who were. On the contrary, they seem to act as if there were no such thing as disturbing the peace or public drunkenness.

"Hey!" someone shouted. "Hey, watch me do the fandango!"

The would-be dancer got up from one of the tables, then began stomping around in an imitation of a dancer. One of the other patrons pulled a pistol.

"You call that dancin'! Maybe this'll help!" He fired at the would-be dancer's feet. His second shot hit the dancer and he fell to the floor, grabbing his foot and moaning in pain.

"Hell, Reub, I didn't mean to hit you," the shooter apologized. He got down on the floor and pulled Reub's boot off, then wrapped the bullet hole with a handkerchief.

The shooting made very little stir in the bar. No more than two or three people even seemed to notice it.

At one table in the back, a bar girl was sitting on a cowboy's lap. At first, Gid thought she was just being a little bold with her flirting, but as he looked more closely he was shocked to see that it was more than just flirting. Gid had never seen anything quite so brazen and he stared in unabashed curiosity.

"Something I can do for you, cowboy?" one of the other bar girls asked, noticing him watching the man and woman back in the corner.

"What?" Gid asked.

The bar girl jutted her hip out and lifted the hem of her skirt, showing naked leg, all the way up to a red garter.

"You seem awful interested in what Mirandy is doin' with her gentleman friend," the bar girl said. "If you come on back into the corner with me, we'll find us a chair, and I can do the same thing for you. It'll only cost you two dollars."

"Are you the one they call Lily?" Gid asked.

The girl shook her head. "No, honey, Lily's not here. But whatever Lily could do for you, I can too. Why don't you come on back here with me and let me show you?"

"No, thanks," Gid said. "I've never been much for doing such a thing in a chair...especially in public."

The girl smiled invitingly and looked at him through cobra-hooded, smoky eyes. "Honey, doin' it in public is what makes it fun," she said. "And don't worry 'bout sittin' in a chair. I'll be the one that's doin' all the work."

"Thanks, but no thanks," Gid said again.

"Whatever you say, honey. You're the one missing out," she said. With one last, smoldering look to make certain he hadn't changed his mind, she drifted away to accost another. A moment later, Gid saw that her solicitation had been successful, as she led a willing partner toward one of the empty chairs in the back of the crowded room.

"Are you going to bet, or are you just goin' to sit there with your thumb up your ass?" Gid heard someone say. When he looked around, he saw a poker game in progress. The one who had issued the challenge was wearing a deputy's badge.

"I'm foldin'," the man who was challenged replied. "And I'm quittin' while I still got two coins to rub together." He raked in the small pile in front of him and stood up.

The deputy laughed. "Findley, what you got to understand is, poker is ninety-nine percent skill and one percent luck. I always did say that's what separates the men from the boys in this game. You are a boy in a man's game."

"Yeah, well, I'll say this for you, Taylor. I never met a man who could run a bluff cooler than you," Findley said. "But you ain't getting' no more of my money. Not tonight, you ain't."

Findley put his money in his pocket and walked away, leaving an empty chair. Gid looked pointedly at the chair.

"You just goin' to stand there lookin', farm boy? Or are you goin' to play?" the deputy asked.

Chapter Five

"Was hoping I'd be invited," Gid said, taking the chair. Having already observed the kind of clientele frequenting the place, Gid sat in such a way as to allow him immediate access to his pistol.

"You puttin' any money on the table, or are you plannin' on trying to get by on your ugly looks?" Taylor asked, and the others laughed at his joke.

"Thought I might start with this," Gid replied. He put five double eagles on the table, and the gold coins glistened brightly, contrasting sharply with the light-absorbing green cloth on the top of the table.

Taylor looked at the money in surprise. "Where'd a farm boy like you get money like that?"

"Is my money good here are not?" Gid replied, without answering the question.

Taylor nodded. "Your money's good here, farm boy,"

he said. "Until I take it, that is," he added, laughing. Then, to the others around the table, he said, "Boys, looks like the farm boy here has decided to join us, so I propose a new deck." Taylor opened a new box of cards. He spread them out on the table, then flipped them over expertly. He was quite good with the cards, and he was making a little show of it for Gid.

"Satisfied with the deck, farm boy?" Taylor asked.

"Yeah," Gid answered. "Deal 'em."

Taylor shuffled the cards, and the stiff new pasteboards clicked sharply. His hands moved swiftly, folding the cards in and out until the probability of random numbers became the law of the table. He shoved the deck toward Gid. Gid cut them, then push them back.

"Five-card draw?"

"Suits me."

Gid lost fifteen dollars on the first hand, folding cautiously with a hand that would have been good enough to win, had he stayed in.

Taylor chuckled as he drew in the pot.

"This isn't a game for the weak of heart, farm boy," he said. "You should've bet that hand."

Gid lost the second hand the same way, and again Taylor laughed.

By the third hand, Gid was down thirty-five dollars, but there was over sixty dollars in the pot, and he had drawn two cards to complete a heart flush. He bet five dollars.

"Careful now, mister," Taylor taunted. "You don't want to get carried away, now. I'll see you five and raise you five."

Gid made a big show of studying his hand carefully. Finally, as if only after careful consideration, he called, but didn't raise Taylor's bet.

"All right farm boy, let's see what you got," Taylor said. The deputy was holding three kings, and he laughed when he saw Gid's hand.

"A flush? You mean to tell me you had a flush and all you did was call?"

"I was afraid you might've had a flush with a bigger card," Gid said. "I like to be certain about things. As you can see, it pays off." Gid raked in the pot. He was now forty dollars ahead of when he sat down.

"It pays off, does it? You're a lousy forty dollars ahead, and you think it's paying off?"

Taylor's vanity was piqued at the thought of a farm boy taking the pot. What he didn't realize was that he was reacting exactly as Gid wanted him to react.

"I'm going to ante the limit this time," Gid said, sliding some money forward. "Ten dollars."

"Well, you're getting into some heavy money now," Taylor teased. "What do you say we up the ante a little?"

"Up the ante?" Gid replied.

"Sure. You say your system's paid off. Why don't we just up the ante and test it?"

"All right," Gid said hesitantly, as if he were being taken in by Taylor.

"That's more like it," Taylor said. He shoved the cards across the table to Gid. "Here. It's your deal."

When Gid picked up the cards, he felt them as he began shuffling, checking for pinpricks and uneven corners. They seemed to be playing with an honest deck. He smiled. Evidently Taylor was so sure of himself that he felt no need to cheat in this game.

Gid dealt the cards. The betting was quite spirited, and within a few moments the pot was over two hundred dollars.

"Now, farm boy, it's time for the nut-cutting," Taylor snarled. "I'm afraid it's going to cost you to see what I have." He slid a stack of chips to the center of the table. "Fifty dollars."

Taylor's bet was high enough to run everyone else out of the game, and he chuckled as it had the desired effect. He looked across the table at Gid, who had not yet folded.

"You stayin'?" The deputy asked.

Gid stroked his chin. "I thought I might," he said. There was a subtle change in Gid's demeanor, one that sent a tiny twinge of doubt through Taylor.

"Well, come on, we ain't got all night," Taylor said.

"What are you going to do?"

"I think I'll just see your fifty and raise it one hundred and fifty," Gid said. He had to take more gold double eagles from his pocket to make the bet, and he dropped the gold coins on the pile in the center.

Taylor's mouth opened and he looked at Gid in surprise.

"What kind of hand do you have, mister?" he asked.

"A pretty good one, I think," Gid answered. He put the cards down in front of him, four to one side, and one off by itself.

"Son of a bitch! He's got four of a kind," someone said. "Look at the way he put his cards down. He's got four of a kind!"

"I'll tell you this. There's over four hundred dollars in that pot," another said.

By now the stakes of the game were high enough to attract the attention of everyone else in the saloon, and there were several men standing around the table, watching the game with intense interest. Even the bar girls—those who weren't working on the back chairs—had come over to see what was going on.

Whispered questions were passed back and forth. Would the deputy call or raise? Did the farm boy actually have four of a kind?

"Call his hand, Taylor," someone said. "I can tell by

looking at him that he's bluffin'. Call his hand."

"It's my money you're talking about," Taylor replied. "It'll cost me a hunnert 'n fifty dollars to call."

"You got it, ain't you?"

"Not to throw away," Taylor said nervously. "Don't forget, this is the fellow who wouldn't even raise a flush."

Gid's face was totally impassive.

"What are you goin' to do, deputy?" one of the bystanders asked. "Like you told the farm boy here, you can't take all night."

"All right, damn it, the pot's yours," Taylor growled, throwing his cards on the table. He had a full house, aces over jacks. "What have you got?"

Gid's cards stayed face down on the table just the way he'd left them, four in one pile, one in the other. He reached out to rake in the pot.

"I said what have you got?" Taylor asked again. He reached for Gid's cards, but Gid caught his wrist with a vice grip.

"You didn't pay to see them," Gid said.

With his other hand, Taylor slid a stack of chips across the table. Gid saw that there were at least fifty dollars in the stack. "Is that enough to buy a look at your cards?" he asked.

"All right," Gid replied. "If you want to." He let go of Taylor's wrist, and Taylor turned up the cards. Instead of four of a kind, there were two small pairs.

"What?" Taylor gasped. "You beat me with two pairs?"

Most of the onlookers had a good laugh, but the deputy stared them down until they were silent.

"You jerked a cinch into me, farm boy," Taylor said. "I don't like that."

"You said it yourself, mister," Gid replied. "Poker is ninety-nine percent skill and one percent luck. I reckon you were a little short on both."

With a frustrated shout of anger, Taylor drove a right into Gid's jaw, taking him by surprise and knocking him back against the table behind him. Taylor wasn't quite as large a man as Gid, but he had a leathery toughness about him, and he was a skilled barroom fighter. He also had a killer instinct, and such an instinct served him exceptionally well in a fight where there were no rules.

Taylor was confident, but he was no fool. He knew he would have to get in a telling blow quickly, so while Gid was still a little groggy, he sent a whistling punch into Gid's Adam's apple, and followed that immediately with a punch to the groin. Gid dropped to his knees, and Taylor drew back his fist for one final, telling blow, to put him away.

Gid saw Taylor get set for a roundhouse right. At the last possible instant, Gid jerked his head to one side. Taylor's hand slid past, finding only empty air. At the same time, Gid sent a short, brutal right against Taylor's belly, drawing a loud grunt and sending the deputy backward with quick little steps to keep from going down. Gid took that opportunity to jump to his feet.

Taylor realized now that he had lost his advantage. His only hope had been to take Gid out with surprise, but Gid had taken the best Taylor had to offer and was now coming at him on even terms. Desperately, Taylor sent a left jab toward Gid, but Gid slipped it easily and countered with a short right hook to Taylor's jaw. It was only the second time Gid had swung at Taylor, but both punches had landed with telling effectiveness.

Taylor tried another left jab, hoping to set Gid up for a roundhouse right. Gid took the jab in order to get in close. He hooked Taylor with a left, then caught him flush with a hard right, and Taylor went down.

Taylor struggled to his feet, but now he had completely given up any idea of winning a fistfight. Instead, he went for his gun.

Gid smiled. He had been expecting this, and he was ready for it. He didn't even bother to reach for his own gun. Instead, he had a clear, unobstructed shot at Taylor's jaw, and he put everything into a roundhouse right which lifted Taylor from the floor, then sent him crashing through a table. He lay on the floor with his mouth open, his jaws slack, and his eyes closed, totally unconscious.

Suddenly the lights went out for Gid, and he fell to the floor, facedown, as unconscious as the man he had just bested. Standing behind Gid were two other deputies. One of them was holding the remnants of the chair he had just broken over Gid's head.

"Big son of a bitch, isn't he?" the deputy with the broken chair said.

"Yeah," the other answered. "It's going to be a load, carrying him down to the jail."

The next morning, Will Crockett, smoking a cheroot and wearing only his hat, stood at the window of the room he had taken upstairs at the Saddle Rock, looking down on Sulphur Springs' Main Street. It was a little after seven, and at this hour of the day, the town had some of the look of industriousness about it that Doc had spoken of the night before.

Two freight wagons, heavily laden with copper ore, rumbled slowly down the street, headed for the smelter. Across the street the storekeeper was sweeping his front porch. A little farther down the street, at the apothecary, the druggist turned the CLOSED sign around to read OPEN in the front window of his establishment.

"What do you see?" Phoebe asked from the bed behind him.

"Couple of wagons, a couple of storekeepers," Will

answered without turning around.

"No," Phoebe said. "I mean, what do you really see? Do you see trouble coming?"

Will turned away from the window. Phoebe was in the feather bed, covered by a brightly colored, patchwork quilt. The quilt held a distinctive aroma: soap, lilac, and a hint of her musk. She had invited him up last night.

"I never look for trouble," Will said.

Phoebe smiled. "You strike me as the kind of man who doesn't have to look for it," she said. "I have a feeling it just naturally comes your way."

"Phoebe! Phoebe!" a man's voice called. Will recognized it as the bartender's voice. "Phoebe, you in there?"

Will reached over to the gun belt, which had lain on the chair within quick grasp all night long and eased his pistol out of his holster.

"I'm in here, Harry," Phoebe said.

"Is Crockett with you? Or did he leave during the night?"

Phoebe looked over at Will before she answered. He had stepped into his pants and was now pulling on his boots. He mouthed the word, "Why?"

"Why do you want to know?" she asked.

" 'Cause there's a fella come into town during the middle of the night that I think Crockett's going to want to know about."

Will finished putting on his boots, then stepped over to the door and jerked it open. He was holding his pistol in his hand and that, plus the sudden opening of the door, startled Harry, and he jumped back in alarm.

Will looked out into the hall to make certain Harry was alone, then he stepped back from the door.

"Come on in," he said.

Harry stepped into the room. Seeing that Phoebe was still naked, though beginning to get dressed, he cleared his throat, then turned aside.

"For heaven's sake, Harry, you've seen me naked before," Phoebe said with a chuckle.

"Not with another man around," Harry said.

"Who's this I'm goin' to want to know about?" Will asked.

"You got a brother named Gid?"

"I do."

"Then you'd better get down to the jail fast. Word I got is, Greenwall's aimin' to hang him."

Chapter Six

"Hello, Little Brother," Will said.

Gid, who had been asleep on his bunk in the cell, opened his eyes. Seeing Will standing on the other side of the bars, he grinned.

"Will," he said. "It's good to see you."

"It's like Ma and Pa told me when we were kids. 'Son, don't take your eyes off your little brother for even a minute,' they said. 'Because, sure as you do, he's going to get in trouble.' They sure knew what they were talking about."

"I reckon they did," Gid answered.

A man, wearing a deputy's badge, overhearing the conversation, came back to the jail cell to see what was going on. The deputy had a black eye and a badly swollen lip.

"You do this, Little Brother?" Will asked, nodding toward the deputy.

"I reckon so," Gid replied easily. "His name is Taylor.

He's not much of a card player, he's a terrible fighter, and he's an even worse sport. Deputy Taylor, this is my brother, Will Crockett."

"Well, Mr. Will Crockett," Taylor snarled, "you got here just in time to see your brother hang."

"When was the trial held?" Will asked.

"The sheriff held it last night, right after we brought him in."

"That a fact, Gid?" Will asked.

Gid chuckled, then shook his head. "Well, you couldn't prove it one way or the other by me. I was out when they brought me in. When I woke up this mornin', they told me I was goin' to hang."

"The hell you say," Will replied. "What'd you find him guilty of?" he asked the deputy.

"I'll answer that question for you, Mr. Crockett," Sid Greenwall said, coming into the cell area from his office. "Your brother is guilty of train robbery."

"Train robbery?" Will replied. "What train did he rob?"

"You ought to know, Crockett. You were on it. Your brother's the one that got away."

"Is that a fact? Tell me, Greenwall, what made you come up with that idea?"

"When we brought him in last night, he had seven hundred nineteen dollars on him."

"It should be over a thousand," Gid said. "Taylor here

took back the money I won from him in the poker game last night."

"The way I figure it, the only way he coulda got his hands on that kind of cash was if he was the fourth train robber...the one that got away with all the money."

"I told him I got the money from selling a string of horses," Gid explained. "He doesn't seem to believe me."

"Greenwall, I saw the fourth man riding off into the dark. It wasn't my brother."

"I'd expect you to say somethin' like that," Greenwall replied. "Not only to save your brother, but also because I'm still not convinced you wasn't a part of it."

"There's an easy way to get to the bottom of this," Will suggested. "All you have to do is talk to the express man on the train. He got a good look at the fourth man. He could tell you it wasn't Gid."

Maybe he could and maybe he couldn't," Greenwall replied. "But the thing is, he ain't here, and I don't have time to wait around for him."

"The way I figure it, this doesn't have anything to do with the train robbery, Will," Gid said. "I figure they have me in here 'cause I beat the deputy at poker."

'It is why they have you here," Will replied. He looked at Greenwall. "Greenwall, they say the robber got away with twelve hundred dollars, right?"

"That's right."

"But you also say my brother only had seven hundred dollars on him."

"That's right too. Figured he's already spent some of it."

"In one night?"

"Don't take a free spender too long to spend five hundred dollars."

"Yeah, well, there's one thing you're overlooking. If Gid and I were partners in a robbery that netted twelve hundred dollars and he showed up here with only seven hundred, you wouldn't have to hang him. I'd shoot the son of a bitch myself."

Unexpectedly, Greenwall laughed. "You know," he said. "You just might be the kind who would do that."

"Damned right I would," Will replied. "And if you hang him, I'm going to shoot you."

"You'd better watch who you're threatenin'," Greenwall stuttered, the smile leaving his face.

"I'm not threatening, I'm promising," Will said. "Now let him go. You know damned well he didn't have anything to do with that train robbery."

Greenwall glared at Will for a moment, then once again he smiled, though this time the smile was more forced than before.

"All right, maybe he didn't have anything to do with robbin' the train," Greenwall agreed. "But he did half kill one of my deputies last night in a fight over a card game."

"Yeah!" Taylor said. "It doesn't matter whether the son of a bitch robbed the train are not. He's goin' to hang for attempted—" That was as far as Taylor got before Will drew his pistol then brought it down sharply on the deputy's head. Taylor let out a yelp of pain, then took a couple of steps back as blood began to run down his forehead, between his eyes.

"What the hell?" Taylor barked. "Greenwall, did you see that?"

"You his wet nurse, Greenwall?" Will asked derisively. "If he can't handle himself any better than this, looks to be like the thing to do is get rid of him."

Greenwall looked over at Taylor, who was now blotting the blood with his handkerchief. The fresh blood added to the black eye and swollen lip from last night made him a pitiful sight indeed.

Greenwall nodded. "You're right," he said. "Taylor, leave your badge on my desk and get out of here."

"What?" Taylor questioned in disbelief.

"You heard me. You're fired."

"Now, wait a minute, Greenwall," Taylor protested. "You can't do that."

"Yeah, I can, and I just did," Greenwall said.

Taylor glared at Will for a long moment before sullenly taking off his badge, then walking over and laying it on

Greenwall's desk. He pointed at Will. "You ain't heard the last of me, mister," he said.

Will took a step toward him and Taylor jumped, then, without another word, turned and left, slamming the door behind him.

Will watched the door slam, then turned toward Greenwall. "May I have my brother now?" he asked, nodding toward the cell.

"You can have him. I guess it was all just a little misunderstanding. No hard feelin's I hope." Greenwall walked over to the wall and took the ring of keys from a hook, then came back and opened the cell door. "You're free to go, Crockett."

"What about my money?" Gid asked, picking his hat up from the bed.

"Oh, yes, the seven hundred dollars."

"Seven hundred and nineteen," Gid said. "Plus, the money I won in the poker game."

Greenwall took a roll of money from his pocket and peeled off seven one-hundred-dollar bills and handed them to Gid.

"Don't know anything about the poker game money," Greenwall said. "And you can count the nineteen dollars as your fine. That is, unless...?" He let the sentence hang.

"Unless what?"

"Unless the two of you'd like to wear deputies' badges.

If you want it, the job's yours," Greenwall said.

"No, thank you," Will said. "I don't think either one of us has ever seen ourselves as lawmen."

Greenwall laughed. "Yeah, I know what you mean. I never figured on bein' one either. But this is too sweet an opportunity to pass up."

"Come on, Gid," Will said, starting for the door.

"I suppose you two will be leavin' town now," Greenwall said.

Will and Gid stopped, and Will looked back toward the sheriff.

"Not for a while," Will answered. "We've got a business to run."

"A business?" Gid asked, surprised at his brother's announcement. "What sort of business?"

"The saloon business, Little Brother," Will said. "You and I are the new owners of the Saddle Rock."

"We own a saloon?" Gid said, smiling broadly. "Well, now, what do you think of that?"

"Are you telling me Edgerton sold it to you?" Greenwall asked. "It's strange that he'd do that, especially after he turned me down cold. How is it that he sold it to you?"

"I didn't exactly buy it. I won it in a poker game."

Suddenly, Greenwall laughed out loud. "So that's how he got rid of it," he said. "Well, I hate to be the one to tell you this, Mr. Crockett, but the truth is, you just got took. That saloon is losing money and has been losing money for a long time. I guess, maybe, you don't know who your competition is."

"Why, it's you, isn't it?" Will asked. "You do own the Bon-Ton, don't you?"

Greenwall blinked, surprised that Will not only knew but apparently didn't seem to care.

"Yes," he said. "Yes, I do own it. And you may have noticed that the Bon-Ton does a lot of business, whereas the Saddle Rock doesn't serve enough customers to pay for the kerosene it takes to keep the lamps burnin'."

"I have a feeling all that's going to change," Will said.

"How do you plan to do that?"

Will smiled easily. "Like you said, Greenwall, you're my competition. You don't really expect me to give away all my secrets, do you?"

Greenwall's eyes narrowed and he pointed at Will. "Crockett, I think maybe I should tell you that I've got things goin' my way in this town. I sort of like it like that. I wouldn't look too kindly on someone who came along and tried to change things."

"No, I don't suppose you would," Will replied.

"It's good to see you again, Little Brother," Will said as the two men walked across the street from the sheriff's office, toward the Saddle Rock saloon. The appellation

"Little Brother" seemed incongruous when one saw the two men together, because Gid, though two years younger, was six inches taller and fifty pounds heavier than his older brother.

"Well, I have to admit I was sort of glad to see your ugly face too," Gid said. "Especially when the sheriff started talking about hanging me for robbin' that train."

Will laughed. "It would've been funny, wouldn't it," he said, "to get hung for a train you didn't rob, when there are so many that we have?"

"Oh, yeah," Gid said, putting his hand to his neck. "I woulda laughed all the way to hell. But the last laugh woulda been on you, Big Brother. 'Cause I've got that train money hidden in my saddle, and you would've never known it."

Will stopped in the middle of the street and looked over at Gid.

"What did you say?"

"That train that was robbed? I've got the money," Gid said easily

"How the hell did that happen? I know you weren't there. I was on that train. There were only four robbers. I killed three, and I saw the fourth as he was getting away. It definitely wasn't you."

"Well, somebody shot the guy as he was getting away," Gid said. "They hit him...and his horse."

"It must have been that Gus fella who did it," Will said. "His own partner shot him for riding off. How did you wind up with the money?"

Gid described his encounter with the robber, Pete Raster, telling how Raster gave him the money as he was dying. "I hope you aren't goin' to say we have to give it back," he concluded.

Will laughed. "Now, tell me, Gid," he said. "Have I ever done a dumb thing like that?"

Phoebe, Harry, and Doc met Will and Gid at the front door of the Saddle Rock.

"Folks, I'd like you to meet my little brother, Gid," Will said, introducing him to the others.

"Saints be praised, he wasn't hanged!" Harry said. "Now, just how the hell did you do that?"

"I appealed to Greenwall's regard for human life," Will said.

"Regard for human life? Ha! When did that son of a bitch ever have any regard for human life?" Doc asked.

"I guess it depends on the human involved," Gid replied. "Will told him if I hung, he would shoot him."

Harry laughed out loud. "Good for you, Mr. Crockett," he said. Then to Gid, "I'm glad you didn't get hung, Gid, but it would almost be worth it to see Greenwall shot down in the street like the dog he is."

"Well, I'm sorry to disappoint you," Gid said, and the others laughed.

"This calls for a drink, on the house," Harry said. "Step up to the bar."

"Tell me, Harry, shouldn't you clear it with the owner before you start giving away free drinks?" Will teased.

"Well, if Mr. Edgerton was here, I'd ask him," Harry said. "But he's nowhere around. Besides, he owes me so much in back wages that if he said anything, I'd just tell him to take it out of my pay."

"That's very generous of you, Harry," Will said. "But the truth is, Edgerton isn't the owner anymore."

"What do you mean?" Harry asked. Suddenly his face went pale. "Good Lord, you aren't going to tell me that Bertie Edgerton sold out to Greenwall are you?"

"What if he has?"

"If he has, then more than one drink is free," Harry replied. "I'll give away everything in the saloon until there's not a drop of liquor left. Then I'll be getting out of town."

Will chuckled. "Relax," he said. "Greenwall doesn't own this saloon."

"Then who does?"

"I do," Will said. "That is, my brother and I do." He took the deed from his pocket and showed it to Harry and the others.

Harry took the document from Will and examined it for a moment, then he showed it to Doc.

"Doc, what do you think of this, is it on the up-and-up?"

Doc looked at the deed and at Edgerton's signature. "It looks like the real thing to me, Harry."

"It is the real thing," Will said. "I won it in a poker game several days ago."

"You mean, when you came in here last night, you already owned the place?" Phoebe asked.

"Yes."

"And you didn't say a word?"

"I wasn't sure how everyone would take it," Will replied. "I didn't know how you would feel about me taking the saloon from Edgerton."

"Mr. Edgerton is a good man," Harry said. "And I didn't mind working for him. But he wasn't the kind of man who could stand up to Sidney Greenwall. If you hadn't won the saloon from him in a poker game, it would have wound up belonging to the sheriff. So, all things considered, I think it's best this way."

"I'm sure Mr. Crockett appreciates your vote of confidence," Doc said. "But how can you be so sure it's for the best? You don't know him."

"Maybe not," Harry said. "But I sure as hell know Sidney Greenwall."

"I say it's for the best," Phoebe cooed. "I haven't known

Mr. Crockett long, but I have, as they say, known him well. He has my vote."

Doc stuck out his hand. "Well, Mr. Crockett, if you can win over these two, then you've got me as well," he said. "Welcome to Sulphur Springs."

"Now, what about that drink you said was on the house?" Gid asked.

"Right away," Harry said, pouring whiskey into a glass. "But, technically speaking, it isn't on the house anymore. It already belongs to you."

"You mean it's already my drink?" Gid asked.

"That's what I mean," Harry said. He slid the shot glass across the bar to Gid.

Gid tossed the drink down, then wiped his mouth with the back of his hand.

"Damn, it's just as I thought," Gid said.

"What's that?"

"Somehow a drink on the house doesn't taste as good if it already belongs to me."

The others laughed.

Chapter Seven

"Harry, if you had to guess, what would you say would be the best way to bring business back to the Saddle Rock?" Will asked.

"That's easy," Harry answered. "Find some way to not charge folks the sheriff's tax."

"Good idea," Will said. "All right, from now on, no more tax."

"If we do that, how are we going to handle Greenwall?"

"Don't you worry about that," Will said. "I'll handle Greenwall."

"I have another suggestion," Phoebe said.

"All right, let's hear it."

"Maybe we could get some of the girls back. A lot of customers like girls to drink with and, uh…visit," she said, searching for an acceptable euphemism. "Before Greenwall we had the best ones, all friendly and pretty.

Then when the business died, they had to leave. A lot of them went to work at the Bon-Ton, but when they saw what Greenwall wanted them to do, most of them quit."

"Why? What did he want them to do there that is different from what they did here?" Will asked.

"You mean you haven't been in the Bon-Ton?"

"Nope. I came here first thing, soon as I got to town."

"Well, uh, I'm sort of embarrassed to tell you what he wants his girls to do."

"Are you talking about the chairs in the back of the room?" Gid asked.

"Yes."

Will looked confused. "I still don't know what you mean. What are you talking about, the chairs?"

"The women over there take care of, uh, their business in chairs," Gid said.

"In chairs?" Will was still confused.

"Yes," Gid said. "In the back of the room…in plain view of everyone, they, uh…fornicate," he added.

"My God. Why would they do that?"

"Greenwall believes that if the men see the girls going about their business out in the open like that, they'll get all excited and the girls will do even more business. And, since he gets three fourths of everything they get, it makes a lot of money for him," Phoebe said.

"Three fourths? Is that normal?"

"I think a normal fee is about forty percent."

Will looked at Gid. "Gid, you didn't..."

"No!" Gid said quickly, answering before his brother finished the question. "Come on, Will, you know me better than that."

"I thought I did," he said. "I just wanted to make sure, that's all. I'm sorry, Phoebe, I interrupted. You were saying something about the girls who left here."

"Yes. I was thinking that if we could get those girls back..."

"An excellent idea," Will said. "Do you think you could get in touch with them?"

"Yes, I'm sure I could."

"Then do it."

"Hot damn!" Gid said excitedly. "Will, do you realize what this means? We not only own a saloon, hell, we own a whorehouse too!"

"Not exactly," Will said, when he saw Phoebe wince.

"Oh, sorry, Phoebe," Gid said. "Didn't mean anything bad by it."

"I know," Phoebe said. She smiled. "And, much as I try and doctor it up with words like 'soiled Dove,' 'buffalo girl,' and 'lady of the line,' I am, after all, a whore."

"Yeah, but you are a good whore," Gid said trying to make up for his blunder. "Uh, what I mean is..."

Will laughed. "Leave it be, Little Brother. You're just

making it worse. She knows what you mean."

Phoebe put her hand on Gid's arm. "Don't worry," she said. "I'm not offended."

"Good. 'Cause I sure didn't want to offend you," Gid said. "Oh, uh, these girls who used to work here. Would one of them be calling herself Lily Bird, by any chance?"

"Yes," Phoebe answered. "Why, do you know Lily?"

Gid shook his head. "I don't know her," he said. "But I knew someone who did know her, and he asked me to look her up."

"Lily is a very sweet person," Phoebe said. "And a dear friend of mine. She would be a wonderful person to work here," she added. "She's very pretty and she gets along very well with everyone."

"See if you can get her, will you?" Gid said

"I'll be glad to."

Will looked at himself in the mirror behind the bar. "If we're planning to have a lot of women in here, then I need to look a little better," he said. "Is there a barbershop near?"

"Leave it to my brother to be the handsome one," Gid said. He lifted his arm and sniffed his armpit, then made a face. "Not sure how handsome I can look, but I could sure smell a mite better if I had a bath."

"We've got a tub here," Phoebe said. "Your brother used it last night," she added as she and Will exchanged a private smile.

"Yeah, I'll just bet he did," Gid said. "Well, lead me to it. I'll see what I can do about getting a little more presentable."

"The barbershop?" Will asked

"Oh, there's one down at the far end of the street, on this side, just before you get to the railroad tracks," Doc said. "The Barber's name is Hugh Young."

"Is he any good?"

"He's the finest barber in town," Doc replied enthusiastically.

Harry laughed.

"You don't agree?" Will asked, questioning Harry's laugh.

"Oh, I agree, all right," Harry said. "Seein' as how Hugh is the only barber in town." He laughed again.

Shortly after Will left to get his shave and haircut, Gid found himself in the back of the Saddle Rock saloon, sitting in a large brass bathtub, happily scrubbing away the residue of his days on the trail. His dirty clothes had been given over to Ling Lee, owner of the laundry, and a clean pair of trousers and a shirt hung across the back of a nearby chair. A cigar was elevated at a jaunty angle, and he was trying to wash his back while at the same time singing, "The dew is on the grass, Lorena…"

"If you'll stop that infernal racket, Gid, I'll introduce

you to Miss Lily Bird," a woman's voice said. "You did say you wanted to meet her."

Surprised that a woman had come into his bath-room, Gid looked around to see Phoebe and another woman standing just inside. The other woman was a full-bodied blonde, nearly a head taller than Phoebe. She had high cheekbones and sparkling blue eyes, and, like Phoebe, she was smiling in amusement at the scene before her.

"Well, now, ladies," Gid said, unperturbed by their intrusion upon his bath. "Are you telling me you don't have an appreciation for fine music?"

"Is that what you call it? I've heard coyotes sing better," Lily said. To his surprise, she came over to kneel beside the bathtub, then took the cloth from him and started washing his back.

"Ahh," Gid said in blissful appreciation. "A little more to the left, if you don't mind. There, that's it, and, yes, I do call it singing. My horse liked it."

"Only reason it never complained is because the poor dumb animal can't talk," Lily said as she continued to scrub his back.

"Look, woman, if it's a job you're wanting, you've a poor way of impressing your employer."

"Is that a fact?" Lily said. She dropped the cloth in the water and stood up. "Well, if rudeness is the way you treat your employees, I'm not all that sure I want to work for you."

"Now, hold it, hold it, let's not get too hasty, here," Gid said. He smiled. "I've never really been a businessman before. Could be, I don't really know how to act."

"It could be," Lily agreed.

"I'm sorry. I'd love to have you working here."

"That's more like it," Lily said. She knelt again, and again picked up the washcloth and began scrubbing his back.

"Ah, that feels good, damned good," Gid said. "You know, Lily, you wouldn't even have to be a whore. You could make a good living just scrubbing backs."

Lily laughed heartily and squeezed the washcloth out over Gid's head, letting some of the soapy water run down over his face.

"Watch what you're doing, woman. You'll put out my cigar." Gid complained.

"And why not?" Lily asked in a teasing voice. "It would clear the air of all this foul smoke."

Gid grinned and dunked his cigar in the water to extinguish it, then tossed it aside. "Listen, have you had your lunch yet?"

"No, I haven't."

"Harry's having his cook fry a chicken for me. Would you like to join me?"

"Harry's going to kill one of his chickens? I'm amazed," Lily said. "The way he fusses over them, you'd think they were his pets or something."

Gid smiled. "Well, now that I'm a substantial citizen of the community, I suppose Harry is trying to impress me."

"And are you trying to impress me?" Lily asked.

"Could be," Gid said. He laughed. "But, Lord, I hope Harry's not trying to impress me for the same reason I'm trying to impress you."

Both Lily and Phoebe, who had not yet left, laughed.

The door opened again, and this time Doc came in. He was carrying a tray upon which sat a bottle and a glass. "Harry said you ordered this," Doc said.

"Yeah, I did. Thanks, Doc."

Behind Doc, a huge, bald-headed man with a scar twisting its way across his flat face came in.

"Your lunch is ready," the cook said. His voice sounded like a train engine letting off steam.

Gid, still sitting in the bathtub, looked up at the growing crowd of people standing around him. "Uh... thanks," he said.

"Mistee Crockett, your clothes be ready one hour," Ling Lee said, coming into the room then. Ling Lee was the Chinese laundryman who had picked up Gid's dirty clothes a short time earlier.

"Now, wait just a damn minute here," Gid said. "What

the hell, is there a sign outside the door saying this is the stage depot? I'm trying to take a bath here."

"Hell, we can all see that, Gid," Harry called mirthfully from the saloon, and his yell was followed by a raucous course of laughter. Gid craned his neck to see beyond the people gathered around the tub and realized that because the door was standing wide open, he was, indeed, visible to any of the saloon patrons who cared to look in his direction.

"Doc?"

"Yes, Gid?" Doc replied, barely able to restrain his laughter.

"Leave my drink and get back to attending sick folks, will you?"

"I will, but this is more fun," Doc said.

"And you, cook, what's your name?"

"The name's Roland" the cook said with another expulsion of steam.

"All right, Roland, you put my food on a table out there, and set it for two. Miss Bird will be joining me for lunch."

Roland nodded, then started to carry the basket of chicken out with them.

"Wait a minute," Gid called, and when Roland stopped, Gid reached into the basket to pull out a drumstick.

"Now, you, Ling Lee, you're not washing my clothes if you're in here. Get back to work."

The man bowed slightly, then withdrew. Now only Phoebe and Lily remained.

"Phoebe, you go too," Gid said. He smiled. "Lily, you can finish washing my back."

Lily smiled back at him and shook her head. "I think I'd better see to it that the table is set for our lunch," she said. "I'm sure you can handle your own bath from here on out."

Barely suppressing their giggles, the two women followed the men out of the bathroom and closed the door behind them. Gid found himself alone once more. He stared at the door for a moment longer, then shrugged, took a bite of his drumstick, and raised one foot to wash, continuing his bath.

As Will walked down the street headed for the barbershop, he passed the Valley Gazette. A sign on the window read: Sulphur Springs's only newspaper, always independent, never neutral. When Will looked through the door he saw a man on his knees, with a screwdriver, working on the press.

"Problem?" Will asked.

The man looked up. "Oh, good," he said. "I was hoping someone would come along. Hold the tympanum for me while I tighten it, will you?"

"Hold the what?"

"This hinged cover here," the man explained.

Will held the cover while the man began making an adjustment. "I am Clarence Watson, the editor," the man said as he worked. "The Washington Hand Press is perhaps the sturdiest press ever built," he continued. "But even it requires a modicum of maintenance if it is to be kept in proper function. There, that should do it."

Watson stood up, moved the tympanum over the bed, and raised it up half a dozen times to test it. Then he wiped his hands on his apron.

"You're Will Crockett, aren't you?" Watson asked. "The one who came in on the train last night?"

"Yes."

"Greenwall offered you a job as one of his deputies, but you turned him down. I'd like to shake your hand for that."

"How did you know that?" Will asked. "It just happened."

"I'm a newspaperman, Mr. Crockett. I have a way of finding out these things," Watson said. He smiled. "For example, I know that you and your brother are the new owners of the Saddle Rock saloon, and that you are not going to charge your customers a tax."

Will chuckled. "You do have a way of finding out things." He nodded toward the paper. "Will you be printing that in the paper?"

"It's news," Randall said. He smiled. "It's also ad-

91

vertising for you, but don't worry, I won't be charging you anything."

"Thanks," Will said.

"On behalf of the citizens of the community," Watson said, "the good citizens," he added, "I want to welcome you to Sulphur Springs. I have a feeling that if you stand up to Greenwall, a few of the others will as well."

"If you and the others feel that way, why haven't you stood up to him before now?" Will asked. "Why have you let him run roughshod over you for so long?"

"You ever seen a herd of cattle being moved, Mr. Crockett?"

"Yes, of course."

"Have you ever noticed how it is easier, sometimes, to get an entire herd to do what you want, than it is to get one cow? See, when a cow is all by itself, it thinks for itself. But when it's in a herd, it waits for someone else to do the thinking.

"I've got a theory that people are pretty much the same way," Watson continued. "Take this town, for example. There are several people in this town who fought bravely during the war. Individually, very few of them are cowards. But put them all together in a town, and they become just like a herd of cattle. No one wants to be the one to make the first move."

"You might be right," Will said.

"Might be? Hell, I know I'm right. That's what happened at Lawrence."

"What?" Will said sharply.

"Lawrence, Kansas. It's a place Quantrill raided, during the war."

"What do you know about it?" Will asked.

"I was publisher of the Lawrence Gazette," Watson said. "I was there."

"I thought all the men of Lawrence were killed. How is it that you were spared?"

"I hid, Mr. Crockett," Watson said. "When Quantrill and his gang came riding in, shooting down every man and boy in sight, I made an individual decision. I went down into the cellar and hid. You didn't get all of us."

"What?"

"I said, you didn't get all of us. I am right, aren't I? You were there, weren't you?"

"Did you see me there?"

"No," Watson admitted. "But I believe you were there. Let me show you something." Watson walked over to the side of the room, to the type-table, then began rummaging through several of the drawers, pulling things out, obviously looking for something. "Ah, here it is," he said with a note of triumph. He pulled a yellowed piece of paper from the drawer, unfolded it, then showed it to Will. The darkly printed words showed clearly through the yellow and the deep creases.

Wanted
DEAD OR ALIVE
The Brothers
WILL AND GID CROCKETT
Known riders with the late Confederate
Guerrilla
QUANTRILL
$5,000 REWARD

"You are the same Will Crockett, are you not?" Watson asked. "And your brother is the same Gid Crockett?"

Will nodded. "We're the same," he said. He pointed at the circular. "That paper has been withdrawn, though. There is no longer a reward out for me."

Watson chuckled. "Not in Arizona," he said. "But I expect you'd still find an unpleasant welcome if you took a ride up into Kansas."

"I expect so. I don't understand, Watson. If you know this about me, and if you were on the other side...especially in Kansas, what makes you so willing to accept my brother and me now?"

"That was then, and this is now," Watson said. "War brings out the best in people...and the worst. I expect Lawrence is something we'd all like to put behind us."

"I expect it is," Will agreed.

"We were on opposite sides in that war," Watson said. "But, from the looks of things, we're on the same side in this one."

Will held out his hand. "Hold on," he said. "I didn't come here to fight in a war."

Watson chuckled. "You turned down Greenwall's offer to be one of his deputies, you've gone into business in competition with him, and you have announced publicly that you will not pay the sheriff's tax. You can't say you didn't come here to fight in a war, Mr. Crockett. Hell, you've started one."

Will smiled. "I reckon I can't argue with you on that," he said.

"You take care, Mr. Crockett," Watson said. "And, if you need an ally you can count on me…and the power of the press. And I promise you, I won't hide in the cellar this time."

Will stared at him for a long moment, then he put his hand on the small editor's shoulder. "About Lawrence?"

"Yes?"

"I'm glad you hid in the cellar," Will said.

Chapter Eight

Gid and Lily were sharing the table Roland had set for them. He looked at Lily, who was smiling back at him. Something, perhaps the expression on his face, cause Lily's smile to be replace by a look of confusion and concern.

"What is it, Gid?"

"What do you mean?"

"You're wanting to tell me something. Have you changed your mind about hiring me?"

"No, I very much want you to work here, Lucy."

Lily gasped. "What did you call me?"

"I called you, Lucy. That is your name, isn't it? Lucy Raster?"

Lily was silent for a long moment, then she spoke in a voice that was so quiet that Gid had to strain to hear her."

"How do you know my name?" she asked. "I don't

remember ever meeting you, and if I had met you, I think I would know."

"I got your name from Pete."

"Where did you see my brother?" Lily asked, the tone of her voice was flat and the expression on her face was one of derision.

"I had built a fire and was cooking my supper when a man came into my camp. He had been badly wounded, shot, he said, by his own partners during a train robbery."

"Train robbery," Lily said, in the same expressionless tone. "Yes, that is something Pete would do. Did he die?"

Gid was surprised by the calmness with which she asked the question.

"Yes," he said.

"Poor Pete. It was inevitable, though. The war changed him. Ma and Pa died during the war. When Pete came back and realized that nothing was as it had been, he rode off to follow the owl hoot trail."

"He died in my camp," Gid said. "But before he died, he asked me to look you up. That's how I learned your real name."

"I have no right to judge Pete for what he became because, look at me. Is his sin of coveting his neighbor's ass any worse than my sin of selling mine?"

Despite the solemnity of the situation, Gid couldn't help but laugh at Lily's self-description, and though he feared for a moment that he might have offended her, she laughed too.

Lily reached across the table to put her hand on Gid's. "Thank you for being there for my brother when he died and thank you for delivering his message to me."

"He wanted me to give you this," Gid said. Taking out a roll of bills, he gave it to her. Giving her the money was a spontaneous thought. Pete hadn't said such a thing.

"Now that you have all this money, you may not want to work for me."

Lily held the money in her hand, looking at the unexpected windfall in pleasant surprise.

"Oh, yes," she said with a big smile. "You could have kept this money for yourself, and I would never have known anything about it. I would be happy to work for such a man."

As Will left the newspaper office, memories of Lawrence, Kansas, tumbled, unbidden, through his mind.

He and Gid walked down Lawrence's main street to move among the dead. They had seen this many dead before, especially after the battles they had participated in, where armed men were locked in desperate struggle against other armed men. But the dead here had not been killed in battle. They had been murdered in cold blood, in some cases, hauled out of their beds while still in their nightshirts and hacked to pieces, are shot down in front of their horrified families while their wives and children pleaded for their lives.

Among the victims were some very young boys, no more than nine or ten, and some very old men, including a few who Will was sure were eighty or more.

And, standing in the street, crying bitter tears over their loved ones, were the women of the town. By Quantrill's orders no woman had been molested, or physically injured. But Will knew that the pain inflicted upon these women's souls would never diminish, and he could feel the heart-chilling loathing in their stares.

At Quantrill's order, the 400 men left Lawrence the same way they had entered it…at a gallop. When they reached the top of a hill about a mile out of town, Will stopped.

Twisting around in his saddle, he looked back toward the town. From here it looked as if the billowing, black smoke from over a hundred burning buildings had collected into one huge column to roil and surge into the sky. And though there was no sound, in Will's mind he could still hear the wailing sobs of the grieving wives, mothers, and daughters of the slain.

"What was the name of that town, again, Will?" Gid asked, stopping beside him to have the same vantage point.

"Lawrence," Will answered. "Lawrence, Kansas."

"Lawrence," Gid repeated. He was silent for a moment. "I want to remember it."

"Why?"

"Because," Gid explained, "I want to remember where it was that I left my soul."

Will was glad to hear that his brother was fighting the same devils he was. That meant that he wasn't alone.

Hugh Young, the barber, greeted Will as he stepped through the front door of the "Elite Tonsorial Salon." The greeting had a salubrious effect on his mental well-being, by ridding him, at least temporarily, of the nightmarish memories of Lawrence.

"Good morning, Mr. Crockett," Young said enthusiastically. "Welcome to my shop!"

"Good morning," Will replied. "Young, isn't it?"

"Yes, sir! Hugh Young is the name, and barbering is the game." He laughed. "Catchy little rhyme, isn't it? Heard that when I was in Dallas, some time back. How's your brother?"

"My brother? He's fine, why do you ask?"

"Most of the town is still laughin' over the way he beat Deputy Taylor at his own game in poker last night. Then, when Taylor tried to make somethin' of it, why, your brother give him what for. Boxed his ears real good,

I hear. Ever'one agrees, Taylor has had somethin' like that comin' to him for a long time."

Will followed the barber into a shop, then settled into the lone chair. "Sometimes my brother gets a little riled up," he said.

"Yes, sir, well, Taylor has got lots of fellows riled up, I reckon. But, before your brother, no one ever had the guts to take him on." The barber held out his hand, palm up. "This shave and haircut will be four bits," he said. "Two bits for me, and two bits for the sheriff's tax."

Will took a half-dollar from his pocket and handed it to Young. "Does every merchant in town collect Greenwall's tax without complaint?" he asked.

Young chuckled. "Well, sir, you're half right," he said. "Ever'one in town does collect the tax, but they don't do it without complaint. No, sir. 'Cause when you get right down to it, why, we have to pay that tax too, ever' time we visit someone else's place of business. But there's nothin' we can do about it."

"There's something I can do about it," Will said. "Starting today, anyone who buys a drink or a meal, or anything else in the Saddle Rock, will not be charged a sheriff's tax."

"You don't say? How are you going to handle that? What are you going to say to Greenwall when he comes around for his money?"

"I'm not going to say anything," Will replied easily. "I'm just not going to pay him anything."

Young put the fifty-cent piece in his cash box, then covered Will with the barber's cloth. "I sure wish you good luck," he said. He tipped Will back in the chair and started wrapping hot towels around his face.

"Luck has nothing to do with it," Will replied.

"Oh, would you like some lilac water?" the barber asked hopefully, holding up a bottle of green liquid. "Only five cents more…well, ten, with the sheriff's tax. And it'll make you smell real good."

"I smell good enough," Will said.

"Yes, sir, I'm sure you do," the barber answered, disappointed at losing the sale. He put the bottle back on the shelf, then started mixing up a lather.

At that moment a shadow fell across the room and when Will and the barber looked up, they saw Taylor standing in the door. Taylor was holding a pistol in his hand, pointing it toward the chair. With a little gasp of fear, Young stepped quickly out of the way.

"I've heard about you, Crockett," Taylor said. "I've heard how you are plannin' on not chargin' anyone any tax when they come to your saloon. Is that right?"

"That's right," Will replied.

"You figurin' on cheatin' Greenwall out of his due, are you?"

"So, what if I am?" Will asked. "What do you care? You don't work for him anymore. He fired you."

"Yeah, because of you, he fired me. I had a good thing goin' till you come along to mess things up," Taylor said. He waved his gun around angrily. "You an' that no-count brother of yours."

"It could be that you had a better thing going than you deserved," Will said. "Maybe it was time someone came along to take that badge away from a mangy piece of dog shit like you."

"Yeah, well, I ain't going to be out of a job long," Taylor said. "Soon as I take you over to Greenwall and tell him how you ain't plannin' on payin' no taxes, he'll want me back."

"You think he hasn't heard that by now?" Will asked.

"Maybe has heard it, but you're still walkin' around free. I aim to take care of that right now."

"Do you?"

"Yeah, I do. Now get up outta that chair." Again, he waved the pistol around.

"Taylor, I came here to get a shave and a haircut," Will said. "If I were you, I'd get out while I still could. Believe me, you don't want to get my dander up."

"What's that you say? I don't want to get your dander up?" Taylor said, as if unable to believe what he was hearing. "Why, you dumb son of a bitch. I'm the one holdin' the gun. If anybody is worried about gettin' their dander up…you should be worryin' about me."

"Leo, why don't you just go along now?" Young said. "I don't want any trouble in my barbershop."

"You stay the hell out of this, Hugh," Taylor growled. He looked menacingly at Will. "That is, if you want to stay alive long enough to shave Crockett's dead ass."

"I'm giving you one more chance to walk away from this," Will said. "I'd suggest you take it."

"One more chance? One more chance? Mister, have you gone crazy?" Taylor asked, puzzled not only by Will's coolness but also by his strange remark.

"Walk out of here now and stay alive. Or push it further and die," Will said. "It's your choice."

Taylor laughed out loud. "Listen to him, will you, barber? I'm the one with the gun, and he's telling me I'm the one that's goin' to die."

The barber took the measure of the two men, then realized something that Taylor did not. There was not the slightest shadow of fear…or doubt…in Will's face. Taylor, on the other hand, even though he was the one holding a gun, seemed to be literally shaking with fright, so much so that it was all he could do to keep the gun steady.

"I've had enough of all this jawin'," Taylor said. "I aim to kill you right here an' right now, while you're a sittin' in the barber's chair." Taylor's nostrils flared, his eyes narrowed, and a vein in his temple began to throb. Suddenly the little barbershop was filled with the sound of an exploding cartridge. The apron that had been spread across Will's body puffed up as a bullet tore through it... from the inside out. The shot left a tiny, brown ring of fire which blazed only for an instant, then went out.

After passing through the apron, the bullet hit Taylor in the chest, tore through his heart, then came out just above his left shoulder blade, leaving a quarter-sized exit wound. The impact of the heavy slug propelled Taylor back out through the door of the barbershop with such force that the door was torn from its hinges.

Though Taylor was already dead, the reflex action of his trigger finger caused his own pistol to discharge, firing harmlessly into the board sidewalk in front of the shop. Leo Taylor fell back, faceup, off the edge of the sidewalk, landing with his head down in a freshly deposited pile of horse dung, while his legs were still up on the sidewalk itself. A spreading stain of blood soaked the front of his shirt.

Will stood up from the barber chair and pulled off the punctured apron. Still holding the smoking gun, he stepped outside to look down at Taylor's body. When he saw that Taylor was dead, he went back into the barbershop and sat again in the chair.

The sound of the two shots brought several people

running to the barbershop. The first ones to arrive were the merely curious, shopkeepers and citizens. Amazingly, none of those who came were wearing badges. Apparently not even a gunshot could get any of the deputies out into the heat of midday.

One of the citizens who came hurrying toward the sprawled body was Doc Tanner. As he got close enough to see who it was, however, he slowed his pace, and by the time he got there he was moving at a leisurely walk. Without even bending over, he kicked at the sole of Taylor's boot.

"What about it, Doc?" someone asked.

"Doesn't take a medical degree to see that this man is dead," Doc said, and there was a nervous ripple of laughter.

"Who shot him?" someone asked.

"He was shot by Will Crockett," Hugh Young said. "Damnedest thing I ever seen in my life. Taylor here had his gun out and was pointin' it at Mr. Crockett. He was about to shoot him when, somehow, Mr. Crockett shot him first."

"Mr. Young?" Will called from inside the barbershop.

"Yes, sir?" Young replied, looking around, surprised that Will had gone back inside.

Will had already put the apron around himself and was leaning back in the reclining barber chair.

"What about that shave and haircut? Am I goin' to get

it or not?" he asked.

"Yes, sir, shave and a haircut, comin' right up," Hugh Young said. But when the barber saw the brown-ringed hole in the apron and thought again of what had just happened right in front of him, he felt a cold fear come over him. A moment later, as he raised the razor to Will's jaw, his hand was shaking visibly. Will reached out to grab him by the wrist.

"I want my whiskers cut, not my throat," he said.

"Yes, sir," Young said. He took a couple of deep breaths, forcing his hand to stop shaking. "Yes, sir," he said. "Your whiskers, not your throat."

Chapter Nine

Sidney Greenwall stood at the front door of the sheriff's office, staring out at the town. Subdued winks of soft light shone from the windows of the houses back in the residential area, while the Bon-Ton and the Saddle Rock spilled golden splashes of brightness onto the boardwalks. The street was noisy with piano playing, singing, drinking, and loud, raucous conversation.

The Saddle Rock, Greenwall noticed, was every bit as busy tonight as was the Bon-Ton. The word on the street was that Will and Gid Crockett were not collecting the tax Greenwall had levied on every business in town.

"Boss, if that's true, and we don't do nothin' to stop 'em," one of the deputies said, "won't be long till ever' other business in town is goin' to be wantin' to do the same thing."

"Is that a fact?" Greenwall asked.

"Well, I mean, I was just thinking…"

"Don't think, Carnahan," Greenwall said. "You ain't smart enough to think."

From the darkness of the street, came the sound of hollow hoofbeats as half a dozen drovers came riding into town.

"Sounds like a live town," a voice said from a distant spot.

"Yeah. Hope they got somethin' to eat in the saloon. I'm mighty tired of trail grub."

"Eat? Not me. I ain't goin' to have time to eat. I'm goin' to get so damned drunk I won't even know where I'm at."

"Hell, Timmy, most of the time you don't know where you're at anyhow," one of the others said.

All the drovers laughed, then rode on beyond Greenwall's earshot.

Behind Greenwall, in the sheriff's office, a few of his deputies were gathered. They were discussing the killing of Deputy Taylor this morning.

"It ain't right," one of them grumbled, just as Greenwall came back inside.

"What ain't right, Cutter?" Greenwall asked, putting a cheroot into his mouth, then leaning over to light it by the kerosene lantern.

"The way Taylor was shot down in the street," Deputy Cutter said. "I mean, the guy who shot him is still walking around, free as a bird. And Taylor was one of our'n."

Greenwall blew out a long puff of smoke, then stared at the deputy through narrow, obsidian eyes.

"He wasn't one of ours," Greenwall said. "I fired him this morning. He started that fight on his own."

"Still," Cutter grumbled, "it don't seem right to let the son of a bitch that shot him go."

"You want to settle scores for Taylor?" Greenwall asked.

"No, nothin' like that. I was just..." Cutter let the sentence trail away, uncompleted.

"Look at you," Greenwall said. "In here, bitching and moaning because Taylor was dumb enough to get his-self shot. I'll tell you this, and I'll tell it only one time. If Crockett hadn't killed Taylor this mornin', by tonight I likely would 've. Taylor didn't have a pot to piss in, or a window to throw it out, before I pinned a badge on him. Nor did any of you," he added. "All in the hell you men have to do is what I tell you to do. Nothin' more, and nothin' less. You do that, and we'll be all right."

"What about the fact that they ain't collecting taxes down at the Saddle Rock?" Deputy Carnahan asked.

"You let me worry about that," Greenwall replied. "All you men have to do is make certain everyone in town respects the law...my law," he added. "And if you can't make 'em respect it...then you damn well better make 'em fear it."

"How are we goin' to make 'em respect the law when the newspaper's a printin' stuff like this?" one of the other deputies, a man named Cox, asked, holding up a copy of the Valley Gazette. "Did you see this article? It's entitled, 'Is Our Reign of Terror Coming to an End?'"

Greenwall began reading the article.

Yet another shooting has taken place on the streets of what was once an industrious and productive town. Leo Taylor, one of the many deputies appointed by Sheriff Sidney Greenwall, was shot down in front of the barbershop this morning by one Will Crockett.

While the death of any human being is a somber event, there are, nevertheless, times when such an occasion is necessary. Legal hangings of desperados are one such example. The death of Leo Taylor is another, for the good citizens of this town well know that it was his bullet which ended the life of Parson Neustadt for no more reason then the playing out of an irresponsible bet.

Although he is not singularly responsible for all the evil which has so recently befallen us, Taylor, as one of Greenwall's deputies, was clearly representative of all that is wrong with our fair town. This writer feels reasonably certain in making the statement that there are none who will mourn his passing.

While it may have been a bullet fired from Will

Crockett's pistol which dispatched Leo Taylor to his appointed rendezvous with the devil himself, in so doing, Will Crockett was, this writer feels, but the instrument of justice.

"Listen, Sheriff, we can't let that son of a bitch go on publishing stories like that," Cox said when he saw that Greenwall was finished reading. "That's the kind of thing that can get people riled up enough to do somethin'."

"You don't worry about Watson."

"I could pay a visit to him now, if you want," Cox suggested.

Greenwall stroked his chin as he contemplated the offer for a moment. "No," he finally said. "No, not yet. First things first. Right now, we have to make certain we ain't losin' control of this town."

At the same time, down at the far end of the street in a restaurant called Helga's, Doc had invited Will and Gid to join him for supper. Helga Glasse herself came over to the table to take their order. She was a tall, strapping woman in her late twenties. Her blond hair was tied back in a bun, but an errant strand had fallen across her bright blue eyes, and when she pushed it back, she left a smudge of flour on her cheek. Her eyes shone brightly as she looked at Gid.

"Ja, do you want something for to eat?" she asked.

Gid ordered.

"Some biscuits, maybe half a dozen, fried taters, maybe a mess of fried onions, and a couple of steaks. You got any pie?"

"Ja, cherry and apple I have," Helga said.

"I'll have a slice of each," Gid said.

Helga smiled. "Ist gut to see a man that eats a gut supper," she said.

"Supper?" Will chuckled. "Ma'am, he won't be eatin' his supper till about eleven tonight. This is just to tide him over."

Helga took the other orders, then left the dining room. Doc saw Gid's eyes follow her all the way to the kitchen.

"She's a nice lady," Doc said.

"I was just thinking that myself," Gid replied. "How come she talks like that?"

"She's German," Doc answered. "She came to America as a mail-order bride to marry some little weasel of a storekeeper. When she got off the stage and he saw how much bigger than him she was, he packed up and left town."

"You mean he run out on her?"

"That's what happened all right. And poor Helga had used just about ever' cent she had in the world just to get over here. When he left town, Helga was broke with no place to go."

"What did she do?"

"She got a job cooking over at the Bon-Ton. But when Greenwall bought the place, he said any woman who worked for him would also have to whore. Helga wouldn't do it, so she put what little money she had saved, and then borrowed the rest from a few people. Anyway, she opened her own restaurant."

"Looks like she's doing all right," Will said.

"She could do better if Greenwall wasn't bleedin' her to death with his taxes. Course, he's doin' that to everyone else as well, so she's not alone."

"Tell me a little more about Greenwall," Will said. "He obviously has everyone in town buffaloed. Just how fast is he with that gun of his?"

Doc took a swallow of his coffee.

"Fast? Well, I don't know. I can't really comment on how fast he is. You can only judge that by men you've seen in gunfights. Greenwall doesn't have gunfights…he just kills people. He can shoot a man in the back as easily as he can swat a fly. As near as I can tell, he has no sense of human feeling whatever…no hate, no love, no fear, no interest in women, no interest in whiskey, nothin'. Killing is as easy for him as sneezing."

"He must have an interest in money," Will said.

"I suppose he does. He's sucking the town dry, that's for sure," Doc said. "But to be honest with you, I don't know if that is as much an interest in money as it is in just watching the town grovel before him."

Helga brought their food then, and as Will ate his supper, he contemplated what Doc had just told him. Fast gunfighters, men who sold their speed, were a predictable breed. Even the worst of them had the common denominator of pride to drive them. Sometimes an opponent could use that pride to his advantage.

It was the cold-blooded killers like Greenwall, who had nothing in common with other men, who were the most dangerous. Will had learned that during the war. He had seen men like Quantrill and Bloody Bill Anderson, and even Jesse James, kill without compunction. He knew such men, even if he didn't fully understand them.

It was crowded in the Bon-Ton. At one table were the six cowboys who had ridden into town earlier in the evening. They were going back south after a drive, but now they were playing cards and getting drunk on cheap whiskey. A cloud of noxious smoke from the strong "roll your owns" they were smoking hovered over the table. The men were playing poker and unwinding from a long and difficult period on the trail. For them, unwinding meant drinking, and the whiskey had not only relaxed them, it had made them quite boisterous. Their presence had been made known to the others in the saloon from the moment they arrived. They laughed uproariously at each other's jokes and comments, celebrated victorious hands, and lamented the poor ones.

"All right, boys, we're down to the nut-cutting," one of the players said. "What you got?"

"I got me two pair, kings and sevens," one of the players said hopefully.

All but one of the other players had lesser hands. But one had a full house, and he let out a happy whoop, then got up and started doing a little dance. His spurs tangled and he fell flat on his back.

"Hey, Gage, iffen your back's too bad hurt, I'll take your winnin's and go get a whore for you," one of the others said amidst the laughter.

"Hurt? You think I'm hurt?" Gage shouted. He hopped up. "Give me your hat. I'll show you I ain't hurt. I'm going to do me a Mexican hat dance."

Gage grabbed a hat and started dancing around it. But, as before, he got his spurs tangled and tripped, only this time instead of falling to the floor, he fell against another table. There were four men at the table, all of them wearing deputies' badges.

"Get away from me, you drunken bastard!" Deputy Dooly shouted, pushing Gage away.

"Hell, mister, you don't have to get your dander up over it," Gage replied. "I was just funnin' is all."

"You're drunk and disturbin' the peace, every one of you," the deputy said. "Come on, you're under arrest. All of you."

The laughter stopped.

"Did you hear what I said? You're all goin' to jail."

Gage shook his head, and held out his hand, as if holding Dooly away from him. "No, sir, we ain't goin' to no jail," he said. "Jasper, you go over there and pick up Timmy." Timmy the youngest of their number, was sitting at the same table with them, but, unable to hold his whiskey, he was already passed out. "Come on, boys, if our company and our money ain't appreciated around here, we'll just leave this place."

The four deputies stood up.

"You're goin' to jail," Dooly said again.

"No, sir. We ain't goin' to no damn jail. Not for doin' nothin' no more'n a little funnin'. I told you, we'll get out of here so's we ain't disturbin' no one anymore. That's goin' to have to be enough for you, 'cause we ain't goin' to jail. Come on, boys, we'll just back out of here, slow and easy-like."

Jasper started over to pick up Timmy as the others began moving toward the door. At that moment the four deputies suddenly drew on them.

"No, mister! Don't do that!" Gage shouted, and, seeing what was happening, the cowboys had no choice but to draw their own guns. Both sides opened fire, and for a moment the room was alive with the flash and crash of gunfire. When the cloud of gun smoke drifted away, two of the cowboys were lying dead on the floor, along with two of the deputies. The remaining deputies were gone having fled through the back door.

"Oh, Lord!" Gage said. "Bunker, Sampson, are you boys dead? Look at them, Jasper."

"Bunker and Sampson is dead," Jasper reported. "Wes is hurt."

"How bad?"

"Jesus," Wes said, his voice strained with pain as he sat down heavily in a nearby chair. Blood was oozing through the fingers of the hand he was holding over a wound in his stomach. "It hurts, Gage. Oh, sweet Jesus, it hurts."

"My Lord," Gage said. "All we wanted to do was to drink a little whiskey and play some cards." He looked over toward the bartender, then toward the other patrons, who were now looking on in wide-eyed shock and dead silence. "We didn't want this. We didn't want nothing like this. How come you folks didn't do nothin' to stop it?"

"Do something, Gage. You gotta help me," Wes said. "I'm hurtin' awful bad."

"Jasper, you help Wes," Guy said. "I'll get Timmy." Timmy was still passed out at the table, unhit by any of the bullets and blissfully unaware of what had just transpired. "We got to get out of here."

"What about Bunker and Sampson?"

Gage shook his head. "I hate leavin' 'em here, but we got no choice. Them deputies is crazy. We got to get out of here."

Suddenly the batwing doors to the saloon swung open and half a dozen deputies came rushing in, all carrying shotguns. The two deputies who had disappeared earlier were with them.

"That's them!" Dooly shouted, pointing to Gage and his friends. "They're the ones who started the fight. They murdered Cox and Morris."

"What?" Gage replied. "What are you talkin' about, mister? We didn't start no fight, and we didn't murder nobody. You started shootin' first. We shot back in self-defense."

"I say you murdered Cox and Morris," Dooly repeated.

"What about our pards, Bunker and Sampson? They're dead too," Gage insisted.

"Come on, let's take 'em to Greenwall."

"A hangin'!" someone shouted a few minutes later, rushing into the dining room at Helga's Café to spread the news. "They's goin' to be a hangin'."

The news fell like a bombshell. Within seconds of

the announcement, everyone in the dining room was rushing for the door.

"What's going on? Is there going to be a lynching?" Will asked.

"Same as a lynching," Doc said. "Though, like as not, it's what Greenwall calls a legal hanging. That is, it'll be legal after he holds court."

"And when will that be?"

"Right now," Doc said. "The one thing Greenwall does believe in is giving everyone a speedy trial."

"How is it that Greenwall is both the sheriff and the judge?" Will asked.

Doc snorted. "The town made him a sheriff; the governor made him a judge. We're just lucky, I guess."

"Come on, Will, I missed my own trial," Gid said. "Let's see what this is all about. I'd sort of like to see how this fella operates."

When Will, Gid, and Doc reached the street, they saw half a dozen mounted men. Behind them, hog-tied so that they couldn't even stand, were four more men. They were being dragged behind the horses, through the dirt and manure piles in the street. One of the four was badly wounded, another was passed out. The two who were conscious and unhurt were shouting and cursing angrily.

"Let us go, damn it! Who the hell are you, anyway?"

The commotion had drawn more people than just

the curious from Helga's Café. They were coming from all over town. Saloons and stores were emptying as the good citizens, drawn by the powerful seduction of instant death, poured into the street. Except for the spill of light from the buildings, it was very dark, but a couple of men had lit torches and were carrying them as they followed the crowd. The four men were dragged for the entire length of the street, until they reached the front of the sheriff's office.

Greenwall was standing on the front porch of the sheriff's office, casually smoking a cigar. When the four cowboys were deposited in front of him, he stepped out to the front of the porch and looked down at them.

"These the prisoners?" Greenwall asked.

"Yeah, Sheriff, I mean, Your Honor," Dooly said, changing forms of address to suit the occasion. "This is them," Dooly said.

"What are they being charged with?"

"Murder, Your Honor. They killt Cox and Morris."

Greenwall took the cigar out of his mouth, then looked out over the crowd gathered in the street.

"Citizens of Sulphur Springs," he shouted to them. "I call this court into session."

"Court?" someone shouted from the crowd. "You have the audacity to call this a court?"

"Who is that brave man?" Gid asked.

121

"I met him today," Will replied. "His name is Clarence Watson. He's the publisher of the Valley Gazette."

"This is a court if I say it's a court, Watson," Greenwall replied. "And all the writin' in that lyin' rag of a newspaper of yours ain't gonna change things. Deputy Dooly, get these here prisoners on their feet. This is a court of law and they got to show some respect."

"They's only two of 'em can stand, Sheriff," Dooly replied. "One of 'em's too bad shot up and the other'n is passed out drunk."

"Very well, then get the two who can stand on their feet."

Gage and Jasper were forced to stand. Wes and Timmy remained lying in the dirt.

"Deputy Dooly, you were in the saloon when this happened?" Greenwall asked.

"I was."

"Take a good look at these here men and tell me if they was the ones who killed Cox and Morris."

"They was the ones," Dooly said without moving from his position.

"Damn it, I said take a good look," Greenwall ordered. "This here court is goin' to be fair. Put the torch in front of 'em so's you can see 'em good."

One of the torchbearers held his light in front of the prisoners. By the wavering gold light of the fire, Will could see the look of terror in the faces of the cowboys.

"Yes, sir, Sheriff, that was them. We tried to arrest 'em for bein' drunk and disturbin' the peace. That's when they pulled their guns on us and started shootin'."

"You're a lyin' son of a bitch!" Gage shouted. "That ain't true and you damn well know it. We was leavin' peaceful like. You started shootin' first, and we had no choice but to defend ourselves."

"What's your name?" Greenwall asked.

"Gage Kendrick."

"You admit you done this shootin'?"

"Yeah, we done the shootin', but, like I said, we was just defendin' ourselves."

"Before the shootin' began, did the deputies try and arrest you?"

"We wasn't doin' nothin'."

"Did the deputies try and arrest you?"

"Yeah."

"You do realize, don't you, that if you had submitted to arrest, none of this would have happened?" Greenwall said. "Cox and Morris would be alive, your two friends would be alive, that one wouldn't be hurt."

"All that happened when the deputies commenced shootin'," Gage said.

"Regardless of who started shootin' first, you was put under arrest and you refused to go. That bein' the case,

Mr. Kendrick, you stand convicted by your own words. There can be no claim of self-defense when you brutally shoot down an officer of the law what was only doin' his duty. I find you all guilty of murder, and sentence all of you to hang."

"What about the one that was drunk," one of the deputies asked. "We goin' to hang him too?"

"Hang him too," Greenwall said. "In my court, justice will be done."

"Court?" Gage shouted. "This ain't no court! This is a city street. And justice? This ain't justice. This here is a lynchin'. You hang us, you'll be doin' murder."

"Take them to the place of execution," Greenwall said by way of dismissal.

"Damn, Will, looks like they're actually going to hang these men," Gid said.

"Looks like," Will agreed.

"Well, are we just goin' to stand here and not do anything?"

"You have any ideas about what we can do?" Will asked.

"No," Gid admitted. "But seems to me like we ought to be able to do somethin','"

At that moment, Dooly backed a buckboard under a large elm tree that stood in front of the livery stable, which was just across the street from the sheriff's office. Immediately thereafter, someone tossed four ropes over a big limb that ran at right angles to the tree trunk about fifteen feet above the ground.

"Get the prisoners onto the gallows," Greenwall ordered.

"Hey," one of the deputies called. He was standing over Wes. "This here'n has died."

"Don't matter none," Greenwall replied. "He's been sentenced to hang, he's goin' to hang. Get him up there with the others."

Gage and Jasper were dragged over to the buckboard, lifted up onto it, then had ropes put around their necks. Next the deputies lifted up Wes's body and connected it. Finally, they slipped a noose around Timmy's neck, pulling him to his feet by the pressure of the rope.

Timmy, who had been completely out of it until now, began gagging and choking. He opened his eyes and looked around, not understanding where he was or what was happening to him.

"You men got anything to say?" Greenwall asked. "Any messages for your family back home?"

"Gage?" Timmy asked in a small, frightened voice. Gage was the oldest, and the natural leader of the bunch. "Gage, what's goin' on?"

"We're about to get ourselves hung, Timmy," Gage said.

"What are you talkin' about? My God! Gage!" Timmy started screaming, and Greenwall pointed to him.

"Put a gag in that fella's mouth," he ordered.

A rag was stuffed in Timmy's mouth, then a handkerchief tied around to keep it in. Timmy's screams quieted, and he looked on at the proceedings with eyes wide in terror and confusion.

"Gage… Gage, they 're really goin' to go through with it," Jasper said.

"Take it easy, Jasper," Gage said. "Buck up and be a man about it. Don't let these sons of bitches see us afraid."

"What about a preacher?" Jasper asked. "Don't we get no preacher?"

"Yeah, Greenwall, how about it?" Watson shouted. "Oh, yes, that's right. You can't get a preacher because one of your deputies killed our preacher."

"Justice has been served in that case, Watson. Taylor is the one who killed the preacher, and Taylor is now dead… as you well know."

"That's true, but you sure didn't have anything to do with it," Watson accused.

"I'm sorry, boys, but there ain't no preacher," Greenwall said. "I'll give you a moment to make your peace."

"Oh…my God!" Jasper shouted.

"Jasper, Timmy, hold on, boys, we're about to take us one hell of a trip. We'll meet on the other side," Gage said.

Greenwall turned to address the crowd. "Let this here hangin' be a lesson to ever'one," he shouted. "There is law in Sulphur Springs, and the law...all laws, includin' the laws about taxes," he added pointedly, "will be enforced." He turned to Dooly, who was still sitting quietly on the seat of the buckboard. Deputy Dooly, carry out the sentence."

Dooly snapped the reins, and the team jerked the buckboard forward. The four cowboys were pulled off the back of the little wagon, then they hung from the tree. Timmy and Wes hung easily, moving back and forth in a slow arc caused by the pull of the wagon. But Gage and Jasper weren't as fortunate. They were slowly strangling, lifting their legs and bending at the waist as if in such a way they could take some of the pressure off their necks.

There was a wail of sympathy and indignation from the crowd, but every man present stood glued to the scene by morbid curiosity.

Will stared directly at Greenwall. Greenwall was calmly relighting his cigar. Then he turned and went back into his office, without so much as a backward glance at the four bodies, hanging from the tree.

Chapter Ten

The town of Sulphur Springs, so wild and noisy the night before, was relatively quiet this morning. Will and Gid stood on the plank walk in front of the Saddle Rock and look down Main Street at the town.

At the far end of the street the mortician's wagon was pulled up under the hanging tree. The four young cowboys had hung from the tree all night, and now Casper Verndam, the undertaker, a tall, cadaverous man dressed all in black with a high hat, had come to claim his prize. Verndam stood beside his wagon watching, occasionally raising a thin arm to point with the bony finger as he gave directions to his grave digger. The grave digger, a strongly built man was cutting down the four cowboys.

He took down the last one. This was the cowboy who had been wounded in the gunfight, and his chest was covered by blood, dried now to a reddish brown. His body was laid out in the wagon with the other three. From there they would be taken to the hardware store where a back room served as the mortuary.

"What I don't understand," Will said, "is why the folks in this town stay around and put up with all this. Why don't they just move away?"

"This is where they were making their home," Gid answered. "It's hard to just pull up stakes and leave like that."

Will thought of their farm back in Missouri, the farm that had been burned to the ground by Kansas Jayhawkers during the war. His and Gid's parents had been killed in the same raid, and their bodies burned with the house. He ran his hand through his hair.

"Yeah," he said gruffly. He spit. "Yeah, I guess I know what you mean."

Will knew exactly what was going through his brother's mind at that moment. In Will's heart, he knew that he would have never stayed on the farm. But Gid had loved the land, loved farming, and had not felt completely whole since that terrible tragedy.

Will put his hand out to squeeze his brother's shoulder.

"You all right, Little Brother?" he asked quietly.

"Yeah, Will, I'm all right," Gid answered. "Listen, I think I'll go back in here and have some breakfast. You want to come with me?"

Will looked at his brother in surprise. "We had a biscuit and a cup of coffee. I thought that was breakfast."

Gid smiled. "That's sure not a breakfast for a working man," he said. "Come on, what do you say?"

"You go ahead and enjoy your breakfast, Gid," Will said. "I think I'll take a walk around town."

"Be careful," Gid warned, as he disappeared back inside the saloon.

Will nodded, then started walking. Maybe Gid could understand why someone wouldn't want to leave, but Will couldn't. What was there about this town that was worth saving? He certainly had no intentions of hanging onto the saloon for any length of time, though he would have to make certain that it was worth something if he was going to get anything out of it. And if the town didn't make it, then neither would his saloon. Viewed in such a way, Will realized that he had a vested interest in the town's survival. That being the case, he looked over the town with renewed curiosity.

The street he was on, Main Street, ran north and south. In the relatively short distance between where he was standing and the railroad at the far end of town, Main was intersected by two streets: First and Second.

First and Second streets consisted only of residences, and though they started out, boldly, as streets... they faded away rather quickly into barely discernible trails at each end.

THE TOWN THAT WOULDN'T DIE

All of the business establishments were on Main Street on this side of the tracks, or on Third Street, which formed the cross of a "T" on the other side of the tracks.

At the head of Main Street stood a white-frame church. The sign out front identified it as a Methodist Church. A black wreath on the door denoted the recent passing of the church's parson. The first business establishment on the east side of the street at the extreme north end of town was the Saddle Rock. Next came the Morning Star Hotel, which had a dining room, then Helga's Café. Because the Saddle Rock also served food, that meant that there were three eating establishments located side by side. As a result, the town's residents, when they could still smile, referred to this corner of town as "Bean Corner."

Once you crossed First Street and continued south there was the feed store, Ling Lee's laundry, and the newspaper office. On the southeast corner of Second Street, there was the hardware store with an exposed stairway climbing up the side, leading up to the doc's office. The last establishment before reaching the railroad was the barbershop.

On the west side of the street, starting at the north end, was the bank, the general store, then the leather goods store. Across First Street was a gunsmith shop, an apothecary, then the Bon-Ton saloon. Second Street separated the Bon-Ton from the jail. In an open lot between the jail and the railroad stood the cottonwood tree from which the four young cowboys had been hanged last night.

At the south end of Main Street and running at right angles to it was the GSR, or the Great Southwest Railroad. On the other side of the tracks set the depot building. Behind the depot, also running east and west, was Third Street. The livery stable and corral, the blacksmith's shop, and the meat market were all on Third Street. Also, on Third Street was the Roman Catholic Church, an old, stone Spanish mission that had stood in that same spot for nearly 100 years before the rest of the town was ever born. Beyond Third Street, about half a mile up a winding road, was the copper smelter. With its huge ore chute and towering smokestacks, it dominated the town, even though it was, technically, beyond the town limits.

Climbing up the denuded mountain behind the smelter was a filigree of flumes and scaffolding, dotted here and there with the scar of pit mining.

As Will walked down the street, he heard a loud crashing noise in the building just in front of him. A large box came flying through the door, landed in the street, then broke open and scattered its contents in the dirt. Clarence Watson, the publisher, wearing an ink-stained apron, ran out of the newspaper office into the street and knelt in the dirt to begin picking up the scattered type.

"Just leave it there, Watson," a gruff voice called.

Three men wearing badges came out of the newspaper office then.

"Dooly, Carnahan, Hooper, I know all of you," Watson said. He pointed to them. "What you are doing is interfering with the rights of a free press. That is a violation of the Constitution."

"No, I'll tell you what's a violation. It's the trash your printin' in this rag you're callin' a newspaper," Dooly said. "Why, this is even worse'n what you did yesterday. Sheriff Greenwall is a patient man, but he ain't gonna put up with this." Dooly held a wadded-up page in his hand.

"Every word is the truth," Watson insisted. "Those men were hanged without a trial."

"They had a trial."

"That was a mockery of justice."

"Well, that's just too bad then, ain't it? 'Cause that's the only justice there is around here," Dooly snarled. He kicked the box, scattering the type for a second time. Watson started picking it up.

"I said leave it!" Dooly said. He had his pistol out and was pointing it at Watson. Watson stood up, shaking with fear and rage.

"Look at him shake, Dooly," Deputy Carnahan said, laughing. "You ever seen a fella shake like that?"

"Looks to me like he's about to piss his pants," Hooper added.

"Haw! Wouldn't that be a sight now?" Dooly asked.

"Please," Watson said to the few who had gathered around to watch. "Someone help me." He saw Will. "You! You're the one I wrote about in my editorial yesterday. You aren't afraid of these people. Please help me."

"You plannin' on getting' involved in this, mister?" Dooly asked.

Will held out his hand. "No," he said pointedly. "This isn't any of my business."

Dooly smiled broadly. "Well, now, I'm glad to see you're comin' to your senses. I reckon you'll be puttin' on a badge and comin' over to our side now."

Will didn't answer.

"Well?" Dooly asked. "You are comin' over to our side, ain't you?"

"He didn't say he was on our side, Dooly," Carnahan said. "He said it weren't none of his business."

"The way I look at it," Dooly went on. "He's either for us, or against us. Right, mister?"

By now a dozen onlookers had gathered to watch, and twice as many people were being drawn to the scene, hurrying down the boardwalk, rushing across the street, spilling out of the stores and business establishments.

Will started to walk away.

"Hey, you! Don't you walk away from me like that," Dooly challenged, calling after him. "I asked you a question. You ain't answered me yet."

"Let it be, Deputy," Will said.

The smile left Dooly's face. "Maybe you ain't gettin' the whole picture here. Now, if you want to be friendly, answer the question."

Will continued to walk away.

"Mister, are you lookin' to die?"

Will stopped and sighed. It had gone the limit now... he knew a killing was about to take place. He felt no hot rush of blood, no fear. He felt only a deadly calm and an absolute assurance that he would come out on top.

He turned around, slowly.

Dooly grinned broadly. "Well, now, I was wonderin' what it'd take to get through to you."

Will looked down at the street, at the type still scattered in the dirt, then he looked back at Dooly. Dooly was still smiling, cocksure of himself.

"Your name is Dooly?"

"Yeah."

"Dooly, pick up this man's type," Will ordered quietly.

The crowd of onlookers was large now, and there was a collective gasp as they realized what Will said.

Dooly laughed a short, ugly laugh.

"What did you say?"

"I told you to pick up this man's type."

"Mister, you talk like you just took leave of your

senses," Dooly said.

"You tell 'im, Dooly," Carnahan said.

"I'm not goin' to tell you again," Will said. "Pick up the type."

"Now, why the hell would I want to do such a thing?" Dooly asked.

"Because, if you don't, I'll kill you where you stand."

Again, there was a collective gasp of surprise, for while Will's gun was still in its holster. Dooly was holding his.

"What the hell, mister, you tryin' to commit suicide or somethin'? You do see that I got my gun out, don't you?" Dooly asked. "And I ain't as stupid as Taylor was. He braced you when you was holdin' a gun underneath the barber's apron. You ain't got no apron coverin' you now."

Will said nothing.

"I mean…suppose I just decided to shoot this newspaper fella and put him out of his misery?" Dooly suggested. "There wouldn't be nothin' you could do about it."

"No, I reckon not," Will said easily. "Go ahead, shoot him."

There was another collective gasp from the crowd.

"What'd you say?" Dooly asked.

"I said shoot him. Hell, he doesn't mean anything to me."

"You…you want me to shoot him?" Dooly asked, surprised by Will's comment.

"Either shoot him, or quit talking about it," Will said.

"You're bluffin'. You think I won't shoot him."

"He's likely to get shot anyway when the killin' starts."

Dooly blinked. "The killin'?"

Will snorted. "You'll be dead, the newspaperman will be dead, and at least one of the two deputies will be."

Will looked at the two deputies. The expressions on their faces showed that they were not nearly as confident as they had been a moment earlier, and yet nothing had changed. Their man still had his pistol in his hand; Will's pistol was still in his holster.

But there was something about Will's voice, something cold and dry, like the rattling of bones in a graveyard. Despite himself, Dooly felt a quick stab of fear shoot through him.

"And what about you? You'll be dead too," Dooly said.

Will nodded. "More'n likely I will be."

"And it don't mean nothin' to you?"

"Not a damn thing," Will replied.

"You...you're crazy," Dooly said.

"Shoot the newspaperman now, and let's get the killin' started," Will said coldly.

"Never mind the newspaperman!" Carnahan shouted nervously. "Shoot this son of a bitch! You got the gun in your hand! Shoot 'im!"

Dooly forced himself to smile, then he started to come back on the hammer of his pistol, all the while moving it around to bring it to bear on Will. He didn't even get it half-cocked before Will had his Colt in his hand. There was a loud bang, and a finger of flame shot from the end of Will's Colt. Dooly dropped his pistol and grabbed his chest. His eyes opened wide in pain and shock. He fell against the doorjamb of the newspaper office, then slid down to the sidewalk, leaving a smear of blood on the wall behind him. He wound up in the sitting position, his eyes open and blank.

"My God, did you see that?" someone in the crowd asked. "This feller just kilt Dooly, with Dooly holdin' a gun in his hand."

"I ain't never seen anyone that fast."

Will looked at the other two deputies. Neither of them had drawn, having felt secure in the fact that Dooly already had his pistol out.

Shooting Dooly had been easy, but only someone with Will's experience would realize that. Will had looked deep into Dooly's eyes and he knew he would stop and think before he actually pulled the trigger of his pistol. While he was thinking about it, Will would be acting, and drawing and shooting for someone with Will's speed was one step, not two.

"Pick up the type," Will ordered coldly.

"Yes, sir," one of the two remaining deputies mumbled.

As the two deputies scrambled to pick up the type,

Will put his gun back in his holster and walked away. He could feel the two deputies' eyes boring holes in his back, but he didn't bother to look around. He knew they would be too afraid to draw.

Later that same afternoon, Deputy Sam Cutter was sitting at the desk in the sheriff's office. Greenwall was next door in the Bon-Ton with Deputy Vince Hooper. Sam Cutter and Roy Carnahan were to, in the words of Greenwall, "keep their eyes on things."

Carnahan was lying on a bunk in the nearest cell. He wasn't asleep, though his hat was pulled down over his eyes.

"You sleepin' in there, Carnahan, leavin' me to do all the work?" Cutter asked.

"What work?" Carnahan replied.

"Hell, you heard what Greenwall told us. He said we was to keep an eye on things. How you goin' to keep an eye on things if they're both shut and covered with that hat?"

"You do it for me."

Cutter chuckled. "Like I said, you're leavin' me to do all the work."

"I been thinkin'," Carnahan said.

"Knowin' you, that's hard-enough work," Cutter answered. "What you been thinkin' about?"

"'Pears like we're getting' our numbers whittled down right good. I mean first it was Deputy Taylor who got killed, then Morris and Cox, now Dooly."

"It don't bother me none," Cutter replied. "The way I look at it, the fewer of us there are, the bigger the piece of the pie."

"It don't bother you none, huh? Well, that's 'cause you didn't see that Crockett fella in action. I did."

"He was lucky, that's all," Cutter said. "They's nobody so good he could do what you said he done...not without he had some luck."

"No, he wasn't lucky. He was good," Carnahan said. "He's the best I ever seen."

"That's because you've never seen the best," a low, hissing voice said.

Neither Cutter nor Carnahan had heard the man come in. Startled, Carnahan sat up on the bunk in the cell and found himself looking at the whitest man he had ever seen. The man's skin and hair were without color, and his eyes were a pale pink.

"My God, who are you?" Cutter asked.

"The name is Black... George Black."

"Black?" Carnahan said. He laughed out loud and pointed. "Your name is Black?"

"Yes," Black said. "What's so funny about my name?"

"Well, I mean...can't you see the..." Carnahan started, then, seeing that the man had no sense of humor whatever, the laughter died in his throat. "Never mind. What, uh, can we do for you, Mr. Black?"

"I'm here to see Greenwall."

"He's not here right now, he's –"

"You. Go get him," Black said to Cutter.

"Now, hold on here! Who do you think you are, ordering me..." Cutter started, then, as with Carnahan before, the comment went unfinished. There was something about this man that generated a primordial sense of fear. Looking into those cold, pink eyes, Cutter could almost believe he was looking into his own grave. He cleared his throat. "All right," he said. "You wait here. I'll get him for you."

"The Albino is here?" Greenwall said when Cutter took him the message. "Good, I was hoping he would come. I sent for him, but I wasn't sure."

"Sheriff, do you know this man?"

"Yes, I know him. I knew him back in West Texas."

"He's a... strange sort of duck, isn't he?"

"He's an albino."

Cutter shook his head. "No," he said. "No, I don't mean that."

"Then what do you mean?"

"I don't know," Cutter admitted. "I don't know what I mean. I only know that I don't intend to spend much time around him."

Chapter Eleven

Phoebe was sitting at a table in a small room at the back of the saloon, drinking coffee, when Will came in.

"Evenin'," Will said. Seeing the coffee pot on the stove, he asked, "Mind if I pour myself a cup of coffee and join you?"

Phoebe smiled at him. "You'd be welcome company," she said.

Will poured himself a cup, then sat down across from her. He took a drink, slurping the coffee through extended lips to keep from burning them.

"Did they get those poor boys buried?" Phoebe asked.

"Yes."

"Those poor boys, buried here in a strange graveyard in a strange town, their fate unknown to anyone who knew or loved them."

"Every man who ever goes on the trail faces that

possibility," Will said. "Take Gid or me. One or both of us could be lyin' in a grave anywhere between here and Missouri. That's the fate of the wandering man."

"Yes, but you're not a wandering man anymore," Phoebe said.

Will took another swallow of his coffee and stared at her over the cup. "Why do you think that?"

"Well, you're here now, and you're a property owner," she said. "Surely you'll stay."

"I'll stay until the Saddle Rock is on its feet again," he said. "Then I intend to sell out."

"Sell out? To who?"

"I thought maybe to Harry," Will said. He paused for a moment. "And to you," he added.

"To me?"

"If you'd be interested."

Phoebe drummed her fingers on the table for a moment or two, then she nodded. "Yes," she said. "Yes, I just might be. Although, without you, I don't see how we can make a go of it. Not as long as Greenwall is running the town."

"I have a feeling things won't be going his way too much longer," Will said.

"Why do you think that?"

"When the others in town see that we don't intend to pay his tax, they'll stop paying him as well. And if a few more stop, then a few more, it will spread until the entire town revolts."

Phoebe shook her head. "I don't think so," she said. "You're the only one who has the courage to do anything. They're all waiting on you to get rid of Greenwall."

"If I did get rid of him, there would just be someone else right behind him, ready to take his place," Will said. "If the people want this town back, they are going to have to take it back. I don't mind getting them started...but it's something they have to do for themselves."

After Will left, Phoebe got a pencil and paper and began doing some figuring. She worked for about half an hour before she came up with what she believed to be a workable plan. If Harry agreed with her, then she and Harry could go into business together, and they could buy the Saddle Rock from Will.

The more she thought about it, the more practical the plan seemed to her, and she actually found herself growing excited about it. She took her figures to Harry, and after some discussion, they decided they would accept Will's proposal.

"Of course, that all depends on whether or not we can live with Greenwall after Will is gone," Harry said.

"I agree," Phoebe said. "But, like Will said, if we depend on him to get rid of Greenwall, we'll just be the victims of the next son of a bitch who comes along."

"That's true," Harry agreed. He sighed. "I just hope we can convince the other folks in town that we're going to have to take matters into our own hands."

"They'll come around, Harry," Phoebe said. "You'll see. They'll come around."

For the rest of the day, Phoebe thought of the possibilities that had been opened up to her by Will's offer. It would be nice to be a property holder, and a woman of some means. She, Phoebe Cousins, could even buy herself a house and move out of the room she had upstairs. On the downside, however it would mean that Will would be leaving. And even though she realized that there was really no chance of anything ever developing between the two of them, it would have been nice to keep him around. But she knew she could no sooner do that than she could cage an eagle.

"What did I tell you?" Watson asked Young, Caswell, and Levy. "Didn't I tell you the Lord would provide us with someone?"

"And you think Crockett is this someone?" Caswell asked.

"Yes. Don't you?"

"I agree that he is someone who's obviously not afraid of Sheriff Greenwall," Caswell said. "But is he someone who's willing to lay it on the line for us?"

"How can you say that? He made Carnahan and Hooper pick up the type after they had scattered it in the street."

"Yes," Caswell said, "after he told Dooly to shoot you."

"I have to admit, that gave me cause to worry when he said that, but I've been thinking about it and I know now what he was doing."

"What?"

"He was taking away Dooly's one weapon. If you recall, he also told Dooly that he expected to be killed as well. I guess he figured if he could put his life on the line, he could put my life on the line too. It was, if I may be honest about it...an invigorating experience."

"He is a cool customer, all right," Young said. "And if you get right down to it, it doesn't matter whether he sticks up for us or not."

"What do you mean by that?" Caswell asked.

"Well...he is one of us now," Young said. "After all, he now owns the Saddle Rock saloon. So, if he stands up to Greenwall for himself, he is, in effect, standing up for all of us."

"You may have a point, Hugh," Watson said. "But what I would like to do is call another meeting of the merchants, this time including Crockett."

"How will we get him to come?" Caswell asked. "I mean, after all, we need him...he doesn't need us."

"There is an old saying," Watson replied. "If the

mountain won't come to Mohammed, Mohammed will go to the mountain."

"What the hell does that mean?" Young asked.

"We'll hold the meeting in the Saddle Rock," Watson said with a satisfied smile.

It didn't take long for Greenwall's new deputy to make his presence known. When "The Albino," as he was universally called, walked up and down the street of the little town, people shuddered involuntarily at the very sight of him.

"Mama, look at that strange man," a ten-year-old girl said to her mother, when they encountered him on the boardwalk in front of the general store.

The girl's mother put her arms around her daughter and pulled her face into her apron. "Don't look at him, girl," she hissed.

"Why not?" the young girl's muffled voice asked.

"If an unmarried girl looks at someone like that, her milk will turn sour at the birth of her first baby," the mother replied.

Others had their own superstitions about him, saying he had been "touched by Satan," and some even insisted that they could smell a hint of sulfur when they passed by him.

His very appearance was so frightening that people

went out of their way to avoid him. Thus, it was nearly a week before the first incident.

The Albino was sitting at a table in the back of the Bon-Ton, nursing a drink and playing a game of "Old Sol." It was fitting that he would be playing solitaire, for he was nearly always alone. None of the girls who worked in the saloon would approach him, none of the customers wanted anything to do with him, and even Greenwall's other deputies tended to avoid him. But if being alone bothered The Albino, it didn't show. The second card down was a red nine and there was a black ten on the board. The Albino played the red nine.

The batwing doors swung open and a cowboy came in. He walked up to the bar.

"Let me have a whiskey," he said.

"Sure thing, mister," the bartender answered, filling a glass and pushing it toward him.

The cowboy tossed the drink down, wiped his mouth with the back of his hand, then turned to look out over the saloon.

"My name is Kendrick. Tully Kendrick," he said. "That name mean anything to anyone here?"

Kendrick waited for a long moment to see if anyone would respond. When no one did, he went on: "Me an' my brother owned a spread some miles south of here. His name was Gage. Gage Kendrick. How about that name?

148

Does it mean anything? I would hope some of you would at least remember his name."

When there was still no response, he continued. "Coupl a' weeks ago, my brother an' some of our hands was comin' back through this town when they run into a little trouble."

Kendrick reached for the bottle and poured himself a second drink.

"In any other town they would have been put in jail overnight and allowed to sober up. The next mornin' they would've paid their fines and gone home." He was quiet for a moment, and so was the saloon, for there wasn't a person present who didn't know now who and what he was talking about.

"But not in this...this hellhole you call a town," he said. "In this place my brother...and the others with him, were murdered."

Still, no one answered.

"I'm told there was a drumhead trial, conducted by someone named Greenwall. I'm told he calls himself a sheriff and a judge. Well, I want to see that man."

"What do you want to see him for?" The Albino asked, his words a low hiss. He had not yet risen from the table, and even as he asked the question he didn't look up, as he was seemingly intent on studying the cards in front of him.

"I want Greenwall to look me in the face," Tully Kendrick said. "I want him to look me right in the eyes. I want him to see the man who is going to kill him."

"Are you threatening the sheriff?" The Albino asked. In the week he had been here, The Albino had said very little. That he was engaged in a dialogue now was both fascinating...and frightening.

"No," Kendrick replied defiantly. He walked over to stand in front of the table. "I'm threatening the low-down sorry son of a bitch who calls himself the sheriff. And that goes for anyone who calls himself a law man in this town."

Now The Albino looked up and Kendrick got a clear look at him. He gasped in surprise as he found himself looking into the expressionless, pink eyes of a face that was as white and cold as death.

"I call myself a lawman," The Albino said quietly.

"Are you...are you Greenwall?" Kendrick asked. Everyone could read exactly what he was thinking. He was wondering if the last being his brother saw on earth was this apparition.

The Albino shook his head. "I am one of his deputies."

Kendrick almost breathed a sigh of relief. "I don't want to talk to you," he said. "I want to talk to the sheriff."

"I believe you said that your threat was directed to anyone who calls himself a lawman. That means your threat was directed at me. Before you see the sheriff, seems like you and me have somethin' to settle."

Kendrick licked his lips nervously. He had come to Sulphur Springs with the twin adrenaline-surging emotions of hate and anger. Now that he was here, and face-to-face with the situation, the hate and anger was being replaced by fear. He began to have second thoughts.

"No," he finally said. "We don't have nothin' to settle. I guess I'll just…let it go, for now."

Kendrick turned and started walking away, feeling all eyes on him, fighting against the urge to break into a run.

Someone began to laugh quietly, and near him another joined in, then another, and another still, until within less than half a minute, the entire saloon was roaring with laughter.

"Hey, cowboy, what the hell did you come all this distance for? Just to turn tail and run?" someone taunted.

"Mister, if you try and step through that door, I'll kill you," The Albino said.

Kendrick froze in his tracks, then he lifted his hands.

"I… I don't want no trouble, Deputy," he said. "All I wanted to do is talk to the sheriff about my brother."

"I believe you said that you wanted him to look into the eyes of the man who was going to kill him," The Albino said.

"I was just talkin'," Kendrick said.

"Turn around."

Kendrick didn't move.

"I said, turn around."

Kendrick, still holding his hands up, shook his head. "No," he said. "If I turn around, you'll try and goad me into a fight. Well, I ain't goin' to do it. And I don't believe you want to shoot me in the back in front of all these people."

Suddenly, and shockingly, the room was filled with the roar of a gunshot. There were yells of alarm and surprise as a little spray of blood flew out from the side of Kendrick's head.

"Son of a bitch! He shot him!" someone shouted.

Kendrick cried out in pain and slapped his hand to the side of his head. Blood spilled through his fingers, and when he pulled his hand away, everyone saw what had really happened. The lobe of Kendrick's right ear was a mangled and bloody piece of flesh.

"He shot off his earlobe! My God, have you ever seen shootin' like that?" one of the awed spectators asked aloud.

"Turn around," The Albino said again.

"N-no," Kendrick stammered. "I ain't goin' to turn around and let you kill me."

The Albino shot again, and this time the tip of the little finger on Kendrick's left hand was blown away.

With another shout of pain, Kendrick grabbed his left hand.

"Turn around, or I'll find something else to shoot," The Albino ordered again, his voice no louder this time than it had been on any of the previous times.

Shaking, Kendrick turned around.

The Albino, who had not yet stood up from the table, put his pistol back in his holster.

"Now, draw," he said.

Kendrick, in tears now, shook his head. "No," he said. "No, I won't draw on you."

"I'm sitting down," The Albino mocked. "How fast can I be if I am sitting down?"

"I'm not going to draw," Kendrick said again, "and there is nothing you can do that will make me."

Slowly, The Albino took out his pistol and aimed it at Kendrick. Kendrick, with tears tracking down his cheeks from tightly closed eyes, just stood there, shaking violently, as he waited for the bullet.

Those in the saloon held their breath, thinking they were about to see an execution. But when the shot came, the ball struck Kendrick in the kneecap. He went down in agony with both hands, including the bloody left hand, clasped across his shattered knee.

"Get up," The Albino said.

"I... I can't get up, you son of a bitch!" Kendrick said through teeth clenched in pain. "You shot off my kneecap!"

"Someone help him up."

When no one moved, The Albino looked up at two

men who were standing closest to Kendrick's writhing form. He fixed them with his cold, emotionless, pink eyes.

"I said help him up."

The two men went over to Kendrick, then, against his protests, pulled him to his feet.

"I... I can't stand," Kendrick said.

"Sure you can," The Albino replied easily. "You still got one good knee...and I'll let you keep it if you stand there."

Kendrick shifted his weight to his good leg. "What do you want with me?" he asked. "For God's sake, mister, let me go."

"There is no God," The Albino said coldly. "You think if there was a God, He would create someone who looks like me?"

"I... I don't know," Kendrick admitted. It was now obvious that he had peed in his pants, but no one said anything. The laughter and taunting that had followed Kendrick to the door when he attempted to leave earlier was gone now. There wasn't a man in the room who wasn't breathing his own prayer of thanks that it was Kendrick instead of himself who was receiving all of The Albino's attention.

The Albino put his pistol away. "All right," he finally said. "Go."

"What?"

"I said go," The Albino repeated. He picked up the

deck of cards and dealt three out, returning to his game of solitaire.

The two men who had helped Kendrick to his feet now went over to help him back outside to his horse.

"If I was you, mister, I wouldn't come back here again," one of the men said. "Ever."

"My God!" Kendrick moaned. "What kind of town is this? What kind of people are you, that you would let mad men like that wear a badge?"

The two men helped Kendrick onto his horse. One of them handed him his reins, and the other slapped the horse on the rump. The horse started forward at a brisk trot as Kendrick, fighting the pain and nausea, held on.

The two men watched the horse until it reached the end of the street, then they started to go back inside. One of them stopped, and the other looked around.

"What is it, Fred?"

"I'll tell you the truth, Ernie. You can go back in there if you want to," Fred said. He shook his head. "But I ain't."

"I got to go back in. I still got a drink I paid for, sittin' on the bar," Ernie said.

"Leave it," Fred said. He started down the street toward the Saddle Rock.

Ernie hesitated but a moment, then he followed.

Chapter Twelve

"If you want to call a merchants' meeting, yes, I'll attend," Will told Watson, Young, and Caswell. "And I'd be glad for you to hold it here."

"Mr. Crockett, the truth is, we'd like more than just your attendance at the meeting," Clarence Watson said.

"Like what?"

"Some of us have worked out a plan to put together another city government...our own city council, our own mayor... independent of the city council and mayor that Greenwall controls."

"Sounds like a reasonable plan," Will agreed.

Watson cleared his throat. "And, uh, we'd like you to be our sheriff."

"In opposition to Greenwall," Caswell said.

"No," Will replied. "I don't think I would be interested in being sheriff, even if you didn't already have one."

Watson shook his head in resignation. "Well, that's it, then. Without your support, our plan doesn't have a chance."

"I didn't say I wouldn't support you," Will said. "I just said I wouldn't be your sheriff."

"Then, I don't understand. What kind of support can we count on?" Young asked.

"Call your meeting," Will said. "When you get everyone together, I'll speak to them."

Watson smiled broadly. "All right," he said. "We'll meet tonight!"

When Will went into Watkins's general store that afternoon, there were three customers there: a man, a woman, and a boy. The man, who didn't seem to be with the woman, was looking at hats. The woman was over on the other side, unrolling bolts of cloth to examine the fabric. The boy was eyeing a big glass bowl filled with horehound candy.

"Good morning, Mr. Crockett," Watkins said when he recognized Will. "I'll be right with you."

"I'm in no hurry," Will replied. He saw the woman looking at him, and he tipped his hat. She made a point of turning away, but before she did, Will saw the look in her eyes, the little lights which were way in the bottom, that said she was curious. If she had the opportunity and no one would ever find out, she would satisfy that curiosity. "Go ahead, take care of the lady," Will said.

"Thank you. Feel free to look around," Watkins invited.

Will looked at the boy and saw himself and Gid, when they were youngsters back in Missouri. He could remember when they would go into town with their father. There was always a piece of candy in it for them. Horehound for him, lemon drop for his brother.

Will reached into the bowl and took out a piece of the golden-brown, hard candy, then handed it to the boy.

The boy popped it into his mouth.

"You didn't have to do that," the boy's mother said."

"I know. I did it because I wanted to."

"Well, that was very nice of you. What do you say to the gentleman, Robbie?"

"Thanks," the boy said, the word muffled by the candy in his mouth.

"Horehound was always my favorite too," Will said.

"Really? You're not just foolin' me?" the boy asked.

"I'm not just foolin'," Will replied.

"I know who you are," the boy said easily. "You're the one who shot Taylor and Dooly, ain't you?"

The smile left Will's face, and he nodded. "I'm the one," he replied.

"Robbie, come over here and quit bothering that nice gentleman."

"But don't you know who he is, Mama? He's the one who shot Taylor and Dooly. Why, I bet he could kill The Albino."

"Robbie!" The woman gasped. "What an awful thing for you to say!"

"But he could do it, Mama, I know he could." Robbie looked at Will. "Someday, I'm going to be as good with a gun as you are," he said.

"Son, I hope that someday people won't even feel the need to carry guns," Will replied.

"Mr. Watkins, perhaps we'd better come back later," the woman suggested, shoving the bolt of cloth back onto the table.

"You needn't hurry off, Mrs. Sullivan. I have two nice bolts of blue cotton in the back that you haven't seen yet," Watkins called to her.

"I'll be back," Mrs. Sullivan called over her shoulder, and the bell on the door rang again as she pushed through it, dragging Robbie outside with her.

Watkins turned toward Will.

"This is for the boy's candy," Will said, handing Watkins a penny. "You take care of your customer. I'll look around."

Will busied himself with counting cans of beans until the customer was gone. Then Watkins came over to see him.

"Yes, sir, what can I help you with?" he asked.

"You know Harry Connors over at the Saddle Rock?"

"Yes, sure, I know him."

"He, Clarence Watson, Doc Tanner, Hugh Young, and Cliff Caswell are planning a meeting of all the merchants tonight. They asked me if I would pass the word around."

"Are you going to be at the meeting, Mr. Crockett?" Watkins asked.

"Yes, I'm going to be there," Will answered.

"Do you have any idea as to the agenda?"

"Lower taxes."

Watkins nodded. "I'm always for lower taxes," he said. "I'll be there."

Will touched the brim of his hat, then went next door to the leather goods shop to invite Walter Levy. In the meantime, on the opposite side of the street, Gid was making the rounds and carrying the same message. As Will left the leather goods shop, he saw his brother going into the feed store. Within half an hour, every businessman and woman in Sulphur Springs had been apprised of the meeting that would be held in the Saddle Rock that night.

"Sheriff, I got a feelin' somethin' is goin' on," Roy Carnahan told Greenwall.

"What?"

Carnahan shook his head. "I'm not sure, but I've seen quite a few people goin' into the Saddle Rock."

"It's a saloon," Greenwall replied.

"I just seen Helga go in there," Carnahan said. "You know she's not a saloon woman. And Clarence Watson and Walter Levy."

"Yeah," Cutter said. "And I seen Caswell from the hardware store, Kidder from the Feed and Seed, and Young, the barber. Hell, even Ling Lee, the Chinaman, is there. You ain't goin' to get that many merchants together in one place unless they're havin' a meetin' about somethin' important."

Now Greenwall was interested, and he stroked his chin for a moment as he thought. "All right, Cutter, go down there and see what's goin' on," he ordered. "If they're havin' a meeting, I want to know about it. And I want to know what they're talkin' about."

The meeting was being held in the back room of the Saddle Rock. Carter, the blacksmith, let fly a quid of tobacco that made the spittoon ring, while Watkins lit up his pipe. When everyone who had been invited found a seat, Harry got up to talk to them.

"Ladies," he started, with a nod toward Phoebe and Helga, "and gentlemen, thank you for coming."

"What's this here meetin' all about, Harry?" Carter

asked. "I was told it had somethin' to do with payin' lower taxes."

"Somethin' like that," Harry replied. "To be more specific…it's about paying no taxes at all. Leastwise, none of the sheriff's taxes."

"We can't do that," Levy said. "If we do, Greenwall will close us down."

"He won't close down the whole town," Watson said. "He can't close down the whole town," he added.

"I'm not worried about the whole town; I'm worried about me."

"Yes," Watson said. "But don't you see? If we all stick together, then he would have to close down the whole town. And that, he won't do."

"That's it? That's the reason for this meeting? We're just going to stop paying taxes?"

"Yes. As I'm sure all of you know, the Saddle Rock has already stopped paying taxes. I've asked Will Crockett, the owner, to share a few words with us tonight. Mr. Crockett?"

Will stood up and cleared his throat.

"Mr. Watson is right; my brother and I are the new owners of the Saddle Rock. And I'm telling you now… the first thing we did was stop paying the sheriff's tax. You can see what that did for our business."

"That's easy for you to say," one of the businessmen

complained. "The whole town seen how you handled Taylor and Dooly. But none of the rest of us is a gunman."

"No," Will agreed. "But you are citizens of this community. And I want you to stop and think what that means. This country came through a war not too long ago. My brother and I were in that war…and I imagine some, if not most, of you were, too. If you were, it doesn't really matter which side you were on. What matters is that you were fighting for what you believed was right. And how anyone who fought in the war could come back here and let a few outlaws take over their town is beyond me."

By God, he's right!" Levy said. "I was at Gettysburg. You got any idea how many men were killed at Gettysburg? How the hell could I go through something like that…then come back here and kowtow to a man like Greenwall, and that bunch of coyotes he has around him? Why, his entire force of deputies wouldn't make a pimple on the ass of a good soldier."

"I was at Gettysburg too," Watkins said. He looked at Levy. "In fact, Walter, you and I have talked about it before…you wore gray, I wore blue. But both of us did our duty."

"Good for you, Mr. Watkins and Mr. Levy," Will said. "That is just the point I'm trying to make, here. A man like Greenwall has no more power over you than you are willing to give him."

"All right, Mr. Crockett, we're behind you," Carter said. "Whatever you want to do, we'll support you."

Will smiled, shook his head, and held out his hands.

"No, you're missing the point," he said. "I'm not going to do anything."

"You ain't goin' to do nothin'?" Carter asked. "Then, I don't understand. What's this all about?"

"Perhaps I can explain," Watson said, speaking again.

"Yeah, please do. I mean, you got us all together, you get our hopes up, now Crockett's tellin' us he ain't interested."

"That isn't what he is saying at all," Watson replied. "He is very interested. What he's saying is that we're going to have to fight this war for ourselves, just as most of us did once before. It won't work if someone else does it for us. What if we just sat back and let Will Crockett and his brother do everything, fight our battles, and make our decisions? If we did that, we could wind up in the same situation we are now," Watson said.

"Are you saying the Crocketts could be as bad as Greenwall and his men?"

"I'm not saying that at all. I'm just saying we should never again turn so much control over to one man…as we did with Greenwall."

"I hope you can see that Watson is right," Will said. "None of you really know my brother or me. You shouldn't be that anxious to let us handle everything just because it's easy for you. Anything worth having is worth fighting for, and you don't deserve anything if you don't have the gumption to hang on to it."

"All right, so what do we do now?"

"Doc?" Watson said. "I believe you have a plan you want to share with us?"

Doc Tanner stood up and cleared his throat. "I hereby make the motion that this body be declared to be an acting city council, with all powers to create and enforce city laws and ordinances."

"What about the current city council?" someone asked.

"What city council?" Harry replied with a smirk. "That frightened bunch of old men are the ones who got us into this mess in the first place."

"But what you're suggesting here is a revolution."

Harry thought about it for a moment, then he chuckled. "I suppose we are making a revolution. But if we are, so what? If it was good enough for our forefathers, it's good enough for us."

"So, what do we do now?"

"Now," Doc said, "we have to have someone second my motion. Do we have any seconds?"

"I second that motion," Phoebe said. Until now, she had remained silent.

"You can't second the motion, Phoebe," Harry said. "You're a woman, and women don't have the vote."

"So, what does that mean?" Phoebe shot back. "When is the last time anyone in this town voted?"

"Phoebe has a point," Watson said with a chuckle. "We're in this together, so I figure the women have as much right to have a say in this as the men."

Doc grinned at Phoebe. "All right, Phoebe, you second-ed it. Now, the motion has been made and seconded, that we act as a town council. All in favor say aye."

"Aye," several voices said as one.

"It is unanimous."

"Mr. Watson, I wonder if you would act as our mayor?" Doc proposed. His proposal was seconded, so that a moment later Clarence Watson, publisher of the Valley Gazette, became the de facto mayor of Sulphur Springs.

"I thank you for your vote of confidence," Watson said. "Now, as our first act, I recommend that we repeal the sheriff's tax. And remember, this must be unanimous. If anyone goes back on this one...you will put all the rest of us in danger."

There was a spirited discussion over the proposal, but before the council finished its business that evening, the act passed. Every businessman in Sulphur Springs left the meeting with the resolve to pay no more taxes to the sheriff.

For the entire meeting, Sam Cutter had been sitting at a table in the main room of the Saddle Rock. Although he was actually outside the meeting room, he was close enough to the open door to hear most, if not all, of what went on. He heard them make the declaration that they would refuse to pay the sheriff's taxes from now on, and that was the news he took to Greenwall.

"Damn!" Carnahan said. "What are we going to do about that? I mean, if all the businesses stop paying the taxes, where are we going to get our money?"

"They aren't going to stop payin' their taxes," Greenwall said.

"They sounded pretty set to me, Sheriff," Cutter said. "It's the Crockett brothers who have them all fired up. Especially Will Crockett."

Greenwall smiled. "Well, then," he said, "I suppose we'll just have to get rid of Will Crockett, won't we? Mr. Black?"

The Albino had been sitting quietly in the corner of the office, seemingly paying no attention to their discussion. Now he looked up in a silent response to Greenwall's summons.

"Take care of Mr. Crockett for us," Greenwall ordered.

The Albino nodded, then stood up and left the office.

"I don't care if he is on our side," Carnahan said after The Albino was gone. "That son of a bitch gives me the creeps."

Chapter Thirteen

Will was standing at the bar, talking with Harry and Phoebe. Gid had gone upstairs with Lily. Most of the others who had attended the business meeting were, by now, back at their own places of business or in their homes. Doc was sitting in a poker game at the rear of the saloon.

This was the setting when The Albino pushed his way in through the double batwing doors. He stood there for a moment, his pink eyes moving slowly around the room until they located Will.

"Will Crockett!" The Albino said. His raised voice contained enough of a challenging edge to arrest everyone's attention.

Will looked around. "You talking to me, maggot?"

These were obviously fighting words, and the customers in the saloon began scurrying, pushing tables aside and knocking over chairs in their haste to get out of the way.

"I'm here to collect the tax."

"What tax?"

"The sheriff's tax," The Albino said.

"You go back and tell the sheriff we've repealed that tax," Will said. He turned back to the bar.

"The sheriff ain't goin' to like that."

"If the sheriff doesn't like our laws, tell him to go find another town," Will said.

The Albino shook his head. "It doesn't work that way, Crockett. You're going to set a good example by paying the tax, now, in front of all these people."

"And if I don't?"

"Then I'm gonna have to kill you," The Albino said easily. "Draw."

Will smiled. "Suppose we go outside?" he said. "There's less chance of someone else getting hurt."

For just a moment a flicker of doubt flashed in The Albino's otherwise unreadable eyes. He had seen every reaction imaginable in the faces of his victims when he confronted them. He had never before seen one smile. Will's smile unnerved him.

Will turned to say something to Harry. As he did so, he saw something in the mirror behind the bar. The Albino was going for his gun.

Will was fast, and had he been facing The Albino in a fair draw, he might have beaten him. But The Albino was also fast, incredibly fast, and by the time Will turned, with his gun in his hand, The Albino was already firing. Will tried to pull the trigger to return fire, but when The Albino's bullet hit him, the entire upper half of his body went instantly numb. He sent the message to his trigger finger to fire, but his trigger finger was unable to react.

The impact of the bullet slammed Will back against the edge of the bar. He hit it, then slid down to the floor in a sitting position. Harry hurried around from the bar toward him, and dimly Will heard someone shouting his name. Sounds seem to come to him from far down in a cave and, though he knew they were talking about him, it was almost as if they were in another room, talking about someone else, and he was a distant and disinterested listener.

Doc came quickly to Will's side. Will saw him coming toward him, then his vision dimmed, and finally went black.

"How is he, Doc?" Phoebe asked, her voice on the edge of panic. "How is he?"

Doc put his hand on Will's neck and held it there for a moment, then he sighed and shook his head slowly.

"I'm sorry, Phoebe," he said. "Will is dead."

The Albino stepped around behind the bar and took

a bottle of whiskey from the shelf. He poured himself a drink.

"You folks didn't really need a doctor to tell you that," he hissed. "I could've told you he was dead from the moment I pulled the trigger."

"You...you maggot-faced bastard!" Phoebe screamed, and she started toward him.

The Albino pulled his pistol and fired into the ceiling. The sudden, unexpected thunderclap of another gunshot stopped Phoebe's charge, and The Albino lowered his pistol and pointed it at her.

"You'd better stop right there, lady," he said. "If you think I won't shoot you just because you're a woman, then you got another think comin'. Killin' is killin'. It's what I do and I'm pretty damned good at my work."

"Back away from him, Phoebe, please," Harry said.

"You'd better listen to the barkeep, lady," The Albino warned.

Phoebe turned away from him and put her hands to her eyes. She was sobbing out loud.

"Couple of you fellas take that door down," Doc ordered, pointing to the door that opened into the kitchen. "Let's put Will on it and get him down to Verndam's funeral parlor. Phoebe, you want to come along with us?"

"Oh, Doc, I don't know," Phoebe said between sobs. "I don't know if I can take it."

The door was taken down and Will was picked up and put carefully onto it.

"Where's Gid?" Doc said, looking around.

"He was upstairs, last I knew," Harry said.

"Get word to him. Tell him what happened."

"I will," Harry said, looking up. "It's funny he didn't come down when he heard the gunshot."

"All right, men, let's get this body down to the funeral parlor." At Doc's direction, the sad little party left the saloon. "Phoebe, I think you'd better come."

"Doc, I…"

"I need you to come, Phoebe. Can't you do this much for him?" Doc challenged.

"I…yes, of course," Phoebe said. "I'll come with you."

Those who had moved out of the way during the shooting now began to return, and tables and chairs were repositioned as the saloon patrons took their seats and resumed their activity. Conversation started again, but it was hushed and whispered.

Gid had reached the top of the stairs just as the doctor pronounced his brother dead. Seeing The Albino standing behind the bar with a gun in his hand made it fairly easy to figure out what had happened. It was very hard for Gid to do nothing at that precise moment, because all instinct told him to charge his brother's murderer and attack him

172

with his bare hands. But The Albino was armed and, at the moment, Gid was not. To confront The Albino now would have been a very foolish thing to do.

Prudently, Gid turned and went back up the stairs, then down to the end of the hallway, where he stepped through the window, climbed out onto the back-porch roof, then dropped down to the ground. Once on the ground, he ran quickly down the alley until he reached the hardware store. Entering through the back door, he saw Caswell standing behind the counter. Caswell looked up, smiling.

"Hello, Gid," he said. "I was just about to close for the day. What are you doing coming in through the back door?"

"It was quicker," Gid replied without explanation. He pointed to the shotgun rack. "Would you let me borrow that Greener for a few minutes?" he asked.

"Borrow it?" Caswell replied, curious as to the strange request. "Well, sure, I suppose so." As Caswell took the ten-gauge, double-barrel shotgun from the rack, Gid opened a box of shells and removed two.

"Thanks," Gid said, taking the gun and going back out through the alley door. Caswell watched him leave, curious as to what was going on.

When Gid looked in through the back door at the Saddle Rock, he saw that the place was still buzzing over what had just happened. He saw also that his brother's body and The Albino were gone. Quietly and without being seen, he stepped back out into the alley.

Gid moved along the outside wall of the Saddle Rock from the back to the front. When he reached Main Street, he looked down to the south end of the street where he saw The Albino just going into the Bon-Ton. Shoving the two shells into the breach of the shotgun, he snapped it shut, then purposefully strode down the middle of Main Street toward the Bon-Ton.

Gid thought about what had just happened. He had known for a long time that this moment might come. He and Will had faced death many times, starting with when they had ridden for Quantrill. They had talked about it and had prepared each other for it.

"When it happens…" Will had said during one of their conversations.

"You mean, if it happens, don't you?" Gid replied.

Will had put his hand on Gid's shoulder then. "All right, Little Brother, if you want to think of it that way," he said easily. "But in our business, it is much better to think of it as when, rather than if. So, if…and…when it happens, the best thing to do would be for whichever one of us is left to just get on with his life."

At the time, Gid agreed with his brother, and he was perfectly willing to do that now. The only thing was, he knew he would not be able to get on with his life until he had settled accounts with The Albino.

About one minute later, Gid stepped through the front door of the Bon-Ton. From the back of the room, the piano was grinding away in an off-key rendition of "Buffalo Gals." The room was noisy with a dozen or more animated conversations. Gid looked around the room and located The Albino sitting alone at a table in the back. Cards from The Albino's incessant game of solitaire were spread out on the table before him. Gid realized that he must've left the game, then come back to it. That made him even more angry, as if killing his brother had been so inconsequential to him that The Albino didn't even bother to quit his game...he just left the cards where they were.

Although many others in Gid's current frame of mind would have called out, cursing in anger and challenge the moment they stepped through the door, Gid did none of that. Nor did he do anything else to call attention to himself. Amazingly, his arrival was practically unnoticed by any of the saloon's patrons. Almost as if he were invisible, Gid walked back to The Albino's table. Not until then did The Albino look up.

"Ah," The Albino said. There was not the slightest hint of surprise on his face. "I didn't think I'd have to come looking for you. I was pretty sure you would come to me...to avenge your brother. And so here you are, come to test yourself against me. Do you really think you can beat me?"

In a sudden, totally unexpected, and incredibly fast move, Gid whipped the butt of the shotgun around to smash in The Albino's face. The Albino's nose practically exploded under the blow, and the blood that erupted so quickly made a bright, crimson smear against the otherwise chalky-white face. With blood and teeth flying, The Albino was knocked from his chair. He landed flat on his back, and, so powerful was the blow, that he slid for a few feet across the floor.

The blow had also rattled his senses, so that The Albino was hanging on to the narrow line between consciousness and unconsciousness. Gid didn't hit him again. He wanted him conscious. He wanted him to know what was happening to him.

The Albino looked up at Gid in total confusion, his pink eyes swimming as he tried to figure out how he'd wound up lying on the floor, and when he had lost the advantage.

"You want me to test myself against you?" Gid said coldly. "Don't you understand yet, you worthless piece of dog shit? I'm not here for any fight. I'm here to kill you."

Without another word, Gid raised the shotgun to his shoulder and pulled one of the two triggers. At the last minute, The Albino did understand, and his pink eyes grew red in terror just before his face was blown away by the deafening blast of the shotgun. When the smoke cleared away, even the most hardened were sickened by the bloody mess that lay on the floor.

Gid turned angrily to face the others in the saloon. A tiny wisp of smoke was still curling up from the end of the barrel he had just discharged.

"I've got one load left," he said. "If anyone wants a taste of it, try me."

He leveled the gun, then began swinging it from side to side. The customers in the saloon moved quickly to get out of his way, and no one made any attempt to keep him from leaving.

Gid went directly to the stable. With Will dead, there was no need for him to stay any longer. And with so many witnesses to what had just happened in the saloon, he figured the best thing for him to do would be to leave town. In no longer than it took for him to saddle his horse, Gid was on his way, leaving the shotgun behind to be returned to Caswell. Only now did he allow himself to grieve for his brother.

Chapter Fourteen

What Gid did not realize was that his grief was premature. Will wasn't dead, and Doc Tanner knew that even when he made the pronouncement. As he explained to Phoebe when he was able to get her alone, "I was afraid that if The Albino knew he hadn't killed him, he might finish the job."

"Thank God he isn't dead!" Phoebe said.

"Not yet, anyway."

"Not yet? How bad is he?"

"Shh!" Doc cautioned. He pointed to the men ahead, who were carrying Will. "Don't let them hear us," he cautioned. Then he answered Phoebe's question. "The bullet passed all the way through, and I don't think it hit any of the vitals. If it had, he would probably already be dead. The next couple of days will tell the story. If the wound doesn't begin to fester, he should pull through all right."

"What if one of the deputies finds out –"

"They aren't going to find out," Doc said. "No one knows but you. And if you want to keep him safe... and me alive as well for what I did tonight, then you mustn't tell a soul."

"But, Doc, I have to tell Gid," Phoebe said. "Gid's his brother. He has a right to know."

"All right, I agree. You can tell Gid, but no one else."

Phoebe looked at Will's still form, stretched out on the door.

"Are you sure he is still alive? He doesn't look it. I mean, look at him. He is so still."

"Did you see the handkerchief I was holding in my hand when I examined him?"

"Yes."

"It was soaked with chloroform. I gave him a pretty good dose, enough to keep him knocked out for at least half an hour. I thought it would be imprudent for him to suddenly wake up and make me look like a fool."

"What about Verndam?" Phoebe asked.

"What about him?"

"He's the undertaker. He'll know, won't he? I mean, as soon as he examines the body?"

"Yes. He'll know. But don't worry about him. He owes me several favors. It's about time he paid them back."

Doc and Phoebe were following along behind the

men carrying Will's prostrate form, laid out on a door. And they were talking so quietly that although the four volunteers were just in front of them, they couldn't hear what was being said.

By the time they got there, word had already reached Verndam, and he was standing outside the door to the funeral parlor.

"My, what a tragedy," Verndam said. He stepped back from the door and held his hand out in invitation. "Please, take him inside and put him on the embalming table."

The volunteers carried Will inside, then lifted him off the door and laid him on a porcelain table that was surrounded by tubes and tanks.

"That will be all, men, thank you," Doc said.

"Mind if I stay and watch?" one of the men asked.

"Stay if you wish," Verndam said.

"No," Doc interjected. "I want everyone out."

"Doc, I don't mind if anyone watches, it doesn't bother me."

"I want everyone out," Doc said again.

"All right, Doc, whatever you say," the man who had asked to stay replied. "I just ain't never seen no one embalmed, is all."

"I'm going to perform an autopsy," Doc said more gently. "It's the final invasion of privacy, and I don't like anyone around."

"Autopsy?" Verndam said. "Hell, Doc, what you need an autopsy for? I can tell you how he died. He was shot."

"There are other reasons for performing autopsies than determining the cause of death," Doc said. "You men, go back to the Saddle Rock. Drink all you want. Tell Harry the drinks are on me."

The four men smiled broadly. "Thanks, Doc," they said, hurrying out of the door.

Doc turned to Phoebe then. "Phoebe, you might want to find Gid."

"All right," Phoebe said.

"When you find him, bring him here."

Doc walked back to the door with Phoebe, shutting it behind her and locking it after she left.

"Hey, Doc!" Verndam called, the tone of his voice elevated in excitement. He was beginning to examine the body. "Hey, Doc, you'd better get over here. You need to see this!"

"Quiet!" Doc said.

"But, Doc, he –"

Doc turned around and held his hand out. "Please, Mr. Verndam, I know what you're going to say…so don't say it."

"You want to tell me what's going on?" Verndam asked, when Doc returned to the table and opened one of Will's eyes to examine the pupil.

Doc explained what he had done, and why.

"Well, how do you plan to keep such a thing a secret?" he asked.

"By burying him."

"Burying him?"

"Or, at least, by burying a weighted coffin," Doc said.

"You expect me to bury an empty coffin? Listen, those things are expensive, and –"

"Don't worry about your coffin," Doc said. "You'll be paid for it."

Their conversation was interrupted by a loud, inpatient knock. Doc went over to the door.

"Doc, it's me, Phoebe. Let me in."

Doc opened the door and Phoebe stepped inside. She was pale-looking, and the expression on her face was one of shock and horror.

"What is it, Phoebe? What's wrong?"

"It's Gid."

"What about him? Where is he?"

"He's gone, Doc. He thought Will was dead, so he took a shotgun over to the Bon-Ton and killed The Albino."

Doc's sighed. "Damn," he said. "I wish I had been able to get word to him before this happened." He snorted what could have been a chuckle. "On the other hand, if he killed The Albino…all I can say is, good riddance."

"Doc," Verndam called from the embalming table.

"Yes?"

"He's comin' around."

There was another loud knock on the door. "Verndam! Verndam, you in there?"

While Doc was tending to the awakening Will, Verndam opened the door to see who was calling him.

"They need you over to the Bon-Ton," the man at the door said. "Gid Crockett just about blew The Albino's head off."

"So, I just heard," Verndam said. "All right, I'll be right there." He looked over his shoulder at Doc and Will, then added, "The one I got in here sure isn't going anywhere."

The man outside laughed. "Ain't goin' anywhere. That's a good one," he said.

Morbid curiosity had drawn so many people to the Bon-Ton that the crowd spilled through the front doors and out onto the plank sidewalk. Verndam had to literally push his way through.

"Let me through, please, let me through," he said as he worked his way inside.

"Hey, it's the undertaker. Let him through. Let him through."

When Verndam reached the scene, he saw several people crowded around one spot, looking toward the floor. At first, Verndam could see only an overturned chair and the bottom of The Albino's boots.

Greenwall was leaning against the bar, holding a beer. "Get him out of here," he growled, nodding toward The Albino's sprawled body. Someone had draped a cloth across The Albino's head and shoulders. As he lay on the ground his feet were turned out and his hands were by his side, palms up. The pistol was still in his gun belt, for he had not made the slightest move toward it. He had been so smugly confident of his speed and skill with a gun that he had not had the remotest idea that he could be in danger from a man like Gid Crockett.

The Albino's problem was that he thought of his pistol as a work of art, a thing of beauty, and the use of the gun, the ability to draw and fire quickly, he regarded as choreography. The Albino had studied other skilled gunmen. He knew how many men each had killed, he knew the glory they had attained, and he could measure their speed in increments as precise as the blink of an eye.

He knew, also, that there weren't more than two or three men in the entire country who would stand a chance against him. One of those men was Will Crockett, and he had made use of that knowledge, choosing the time to put Crockett down, using the "edge" of starting his draw when Crockett's back was to him. He knew, also, that of the two Crockett brothers, Will was, by far, the most skilled gunman.

It was what The Albino didn't know about Gid that got him killed. To Gid a gun was nothing but a tool, like a shovel, or a plow. Gid didn't study tools, he used them. He went to the saloon with only one purpose in mind, and that was to kill The Albino. And, in the fulfillment of that purpose, he made excellent use of the tool he was holding in his hand, a double-barreled, ten-gauge, Greener shotgun.

The result was the disfigured corpse Verndam was now examining.

Verndam pulled the cloth back and looked at what used to be The Albino's face. It looked like a piece of liver.

"There's no way I can ever fix his face for viewing," Verndam said.

"Hell, no one could stand to look at the ugly son of a bitch while he was alive," Greenwall growled. "Who'd want to look at him dead? Forget about trying to do anything to his face."

"You will be paying for his funeral?" Verndam asked.

"How much will it cost?"

"Well, there's the embalming, and the clothes, and the coffin. I'm sure you'll want the best coffin... and, of course, you'll want to bury him in a manner befitting one of your deputies, so I would say –"

"Forget the embalming," Greenwall said with an impatient wave of his hand. "And the coffin. Just wrap the bastard in a piece of tarpaulin and put him in the ground. And do it tonight," he added. "There's no sense in keeping the ugly son of a bitch around any longer that we have to."

In the next twenty-four hours an interesting dichotomy took place in Sulphur Springs.

In the matter of George Black, The Albino, there was a corpse without a funeral.

In the matter of Will Crockett, there was a funeral without a corpse.

On the day of Will's funeral, the Saddle Rock was closed. So were all the other businesses up and down Main Street. The only exception was the Bon-Ton. It was open, but it too was practically empty, with only four or five customers who weren't wearing a deputy's badge.

"Where the hell is ever'body?" Greenwall asked as he stepped up to the bar. The bartender moved down to him, then selected a bottle from under the bar. Unlike the bottles on the shelves behind the bar, this one had a label, indicating it was a better stock than that normally served to Bon-Ton customers.

"Why, Sheriff, they're all at Will Crockett's funeral," the bartender said. "Haven't you noticed? The whole town is closed up…stores, shops, even the bank."

At that moment the church bell began to peal.

"What are they ringin' the bell for?" Greenwall asked.

"They got to," the bartender replied.

"What do you mean, they got to?"

"Ain't you never heard? You've got to ring the bell the same number of times as the number of years the dead person lived. Otherwise, his soul is lost in limbo."

"Lost in limbo? What does that mean?"

"It means the soul don't go to Heaven or Hell. It just wanders around."

"You mean like a ghost?" Carnahan asked. He and Cutter had been listening to the conversation.

"Yeah, sort of like that, I suppose," the bartender answered.

"Ooooooooohh. I'm the ghost of Will Crockett!" Cutter moaned, and the others laughed.

"Shut up!" Greenwall ordered. He turned away from the bar and pointed at his deputies, and the few others who were still in the saloon. "All of you, just shut the hell up!"

"Hey, come on, Sheriff," Carnahan said. "We didn't mean nothin' by it. We was just funnin' a little, that's all."

"Yeah, well any more funnin' like that and I'll turn one of you into a real ghost, if you get my meanin'." Greenwall said menacingly.

"We get your meanin'," Cutter said.

Greenwall walked to the door of the saloon and looked down the north end of the street at the church. The front doors of the church had been thrown open, and at that moment, six men were coming through the door, carrying a coffin. Gingerly, they came down the steps, then slid the coffin into the back of the hearse. Others began pouring out of the church then, and, within a few moments, a procession was formed. With the hearse leading the way, the funeral cortege started south on Main Street. In just a moment or two, they would be passing in front of the Bon-Ton, then they would turn west on Second Street, on their way to the cemetery. Some of the mourners rode in carriages or wagons, some rode horses, but nearly as many walked.

"Get over here," Greenwall said gruffly. "All of you. Get over here and show some respect for the dead." Greenwall took off his hat.

"Sheriff, you can't be serious. You ain't never showed respect for any dead before. Besides which, you're the one who told The Albino to kill him."

"I'm very serious," Greenwall said coldly.

With a shrug of his shoulders. Carnahan looked at Cutter, then the others who were in the saloon. To a man, they rose and walked over to the front door. Greenwall moved out onto the porch and indicated that they should do the same. Then, as the funeral cortège passed by, Greenwall, his deputies, and the few patrons of Greenwall's saloon stood by silently, with their heads bared.

Phoebe, dressed in black and wearing a long, black

veil, rode in the first buggy behind the hearse. The buggy was being driven by Harry Connors. When Phoebe saw Greenwall and the others making a gesture of respect she looked pointedly away from them.

After the funeral, Harry stopped the buggy in front of the Saddle Rock, then helped Phoebe down.

"How long do you think we should stay shut?" Harry asked.

"I'd say at least three days," Phoebe replied. "Don't you think?"

"Yes," Harry said. "Will Crockett was a good man. A damn good man. We won't see his kind around again, for a while."

In keeping her promise to Doc Tanner, Phoebe had not shared with Harry the fact that Will was still alive. She reached out to lay her fingers on his hand.

"Maybe we will, Harry," she said. "Sooner than you think."

Once inside the saloon, Phoebe walked through the quiet bar area. It was lighted by splashes of sunlight that managed to find its way in through the cracks and gaps of the closed window shutters. Phoebe pulled the hat pin from her stiffened hat and took it and the veil off, wadding the little bits of cloth and stiffener in her hands as she climbed the stairs to the top floor. When she reached the top of the stairs she looked down toward the closed doors of what had been Will's and Gid's rooms, sighed, then moved quickly toward her own room.

"How did the funeral go?" Doc Tanner asked just as Phoebe was letting herself in.

"It went fine."

"Anybody say anything about my not being there?"

"Not that I overheard," Phoebe said. "Maybe nobody even noticed. The funeral was very well attended. Nearly everyone in town was there."

"Well, of course it would be," Doc said. "Most of the people in this town had put their hopes in Will being able to save them. Were you surprised that it was so well attended?"

"No, I mean, I guess I knew there would be a crowd. It's just that, well, Doc, I don't know. I feel like we're being dishonest with everyone in town."

"Maybe we are," Doc agreed. "But we can't afford to let anyone know what's going on. At least, not yet. And when the people find out what we did, and why we did it, they'll forgive us. Believe me, Phoebe, they will forgive us."

"I suppose so. How is the patient doing?"

"He's sleeping. You want to look in on him?"

"Yes," Phoebe said. She walked into her room and looked inside. There, on the bed, his chest swathed in bandages and his eyes closed in troubled sleep, lay Will

190

Crockett. "Is he going to make it?" she asked.

"It's looking better. It's been two days now, and still no signs of wound mortification. And every day he stays alive is one day of getting stronger."

"He's going to make it," Phoebe said. "I know he is."

"Phoebe, I'm going to have to depend on you to take care of all the nursing," Doc Tanner said. "You're going to have to keep his bandages changed, keep them clean and warm. It's going to take an awful lot of hard work."

"Hard work I can provide," Phoebe said. "I don't know about my nursing skills, though."

Doc Tanner reached out and patted Phoebe on the hand. "I have faith in you, Phoebe," he said. "As far as I'm concerned, Will wouldn't have any better chance if he was in the finest hospital in the world. Now, I've got to get out and be seen around town. I'll drop back in to check on him tomorrow."

"All right, Doc," Phoebe said. "And thanks for everything."

After Doc Tanner left, Phoebe pulled up a rocking chair and sat next to Will's bed. She rocked back and forth slowly, all the while looking into Will's face. It was a nice face. There might have been faces more handsome, but none more pleasing to her eyes.

Will's eyes were closed now, but she wished they were open. His eyes were the most fascinating feature about his face. They were deep and dark blue, and when she looked into them long enough and hard enough, she would sometimes feel herself spinning away into dizziness, like trying to contemplate eternity.

"Will," she said softly. "Will, I know you can't hear me now, but I want to tell you that I'm not going to let you die. Do you hear me? I am not here to let you die."

Phoebe raised up in her chair a little to see if her words had had any effect on Will. It didn't appear that they had.

"I don't know where Gid is right now. He killed the bastard who shot you, then he left town. But I can't get over the feeling that we'll hear from him again, and when we do, I'll let him know the truth. And when he learns that you aren't dead, he'll be as happy as I was. And it was almost worth the despair to have that joy."

Chapter Fifteen

"No!" Will suddenly shouted. At the cry, he sat up in bed and swung his legs over the edge so quickly that Phoebe, who had been dozing in the rocking chair, was startled awake. "I've got to warn Quantrill!" Will shouted. He tried to stand up.

"Will! Will, what are you doing? You'll open your wound. You'll start bleeding again."

"Excuse me, ma'am," Will said. He looked toward the door. "Gid, Gid, get in here. Where's Gid? We've got to get word to Quantrill."

"Will, it's me, Phoebe. Don't you recognize me?"

Will looked at Phoebe with eyes that were burning with intensity. "Phoebe! What are you doing here?" he asked. "You've got to get out of here! The battle is going to start at any moment! The Yankees are massing on the other side of the trees!"

"Will, listen to me," Phoebe said. "That war is over. Do you hear me? That war is over. You're safe now. You're here, in my bedroom."

"Your bedroom?" Will asked, sitting back down on the edge of the bed. He put his hand over his wound, and it came away bloody. Will looked around in confusion. "I'm in your bedroom," he said. "What am I doing in here?"

"You've been shot," Phoebe said.

Will looked down at his chest. "Yes," he said dryly. "Well, I may not know what the hell is going on, but I can tell that I've been shot. It hurts like hell."

"Lie back down," Phoebe ordered. "I need to change the dressing now."

"All right," Will said, obeying her order without question.

Phoebe poured some water into a basin and brought it over to put on the little table beside the bed. Gingerly, she began removing his old bandage, then started bathing the wound.

"I remember now," Will said. "It was The Albino, wasn't it?"

"Yes."

Will looked around the room. "What am I doing in your bedroom? Why aren't I down at the doc's office?"

"Doc thought it would be best to keep you out of sight," Phoebe said.

194

"Out of sight?"

"He thought it would be safer."

"Look here, are you telling me I am hiding from that maggot bastard?" Will tried to stand up.

"No," Phoebe said. "You don't have to hide from him. He's dead."

"Dead? Did I kill him?"

"No, Gid did."

"Gid? But I don't understand. As fast as The Albino is, how could Gid…"

"From what I hear," Phoebe said as she continued to work, "your brother just walked into the Bon-Ton with a shotgun and blew The Albino's head off without so much as a fair thee well."

Will laughed, then grabbed himself in the chest. "That hurts," he said. "Yeah, that's the way Gid would do it, all right. He is pretty methodical about things. Where is he now?"

"Nobody knows. As soon as he killed The Albino, he left town."

"Well, he'll get in touch."

Phoebe looked at Will with a pained expression on her face.

"What is it?" Will asked. "What's wrong?"

"Will, Gid thinks you are dead."

"He thinks I'm dead?"

"Doc was there when you were shot. He examined you, then pronounced you dead. That was to keep The Albino from finishing you off. Then Doc thought it might be safer to let everyone think that."

"Didn't anyone think Gid might have a right to know?"

"I went to tell him," Phoebe said. "But before I could find him, he had already killed The Albino and left."

"Damn," Will said.

"I'm sorry."

Will lifted his hand and put it on Phoebe's arm. "No," he said. "It isn't your fault. You and Doc did what you thought was right…and under the circumstances, who is to argue with you? Don't worry, I'll find Gid."

It was mid-afternoon and the sun was a brilliant orb half-way down its western transit when he saw the little town of Pacific rising into view on the plains before him. Sunlight shimmered off the shingled roofs and clapboard sidings of the dozen or so buildings of the town. The tallest structure of the town was the water tower, down by the depot.

Pacific was a busy town. Board sidewalks clattered with the footsteps of men and women who were attending to their daily business, a couple of full freight wagons lumbered down the single dirt street, while, over at the leather company, rendering pots simmered and stunk as hides were being tanned.

Gid rode through the town till he reached the first saloon. There, he tied his horse off out front, then went in to have a drink. Two men, close by, were involved in conversation. When he heard Sulphur Springs mentioned, he began paying attention.

"It was over to Sulphur Springs that it happened," one of the two men said. "The way I heard it, Tully Kendrick went over there to find out what happened to his brother an' his hands, and he got near shot to pieces by one of the deputies they got over there."

"Sulphur Springs? I was over to Sulphur Springs couple years ago. I thought that was a pretty decent town."

"It used to be, till Sidney Greenwall come along. He's sheriff over there now, and he's got hisself a bunch of mean deputies. From what I hear, Sulphur Springs ain't a fit place to live…ain't even a place a fella would want to visit anymore."

"Why don't they elect 'em a new sheriff?"

"Elect? Hell, they didn't elect Greenwall. He buffaloed the town council into appointin' him. And from what I hear, the town council's too scared to even meet anymore, so there's no way to get rid of him."

"That's a shame. There's some pretty good folks over there. Somebody ought to do somethin'."

"Like what?"

"I don't know. Write a letter or somethin'."

The first man snorted. "Write a letter. Abe, you talk like a man with a paper asshole. What the hell good is writin' a letter goin' to do?"

"I don't know," the one called Abe replied. "But seems to me like somebody ought to do somethin'."

"Want another?" The bartender asked, moving down the bar to stand in front of Gid, just as Gid was finishing his beer.

"Uh, no, thanks," Gid said. "One was enough."

The conversation made Gid realize that he should have stayed in Sulphur Springs to finish what he and his brother had started. He hadn't been thinking clearly when he left. He had killed The Albino because the son of a bitch needed killing...then he left town because that seemed to be the natural thing to do.

It might have been the natural thing, he decided, but not the best thing. The best thing would be to go back and help the town get rid of Greenwall. And not just because he was a do-gooder. After all, he had an economic interest to protect. He and Will... Gid paused. No, not he and Will...Will was gone and Gid was going to have to get used to thinking that way. He—Gid—owned a saloon in Sulphur Springs, and he would be damned if he'd let Greenwall take it away from him.

When Gid stepped into the depot, the stationmaster and the telegrapher were engaged in an intense conversation about Lillie Langtry. The question seemed to be whether or not she was more beautiful than Cleopatra. The train master was sure that she was.

"Don't get me wrong," the telegrapher said. "I ain't sayin' she ain't prettier than Cleopatra. I'm just sayin' that there ain't no one alive who ever seen Cleopatra, so there's no way of knowin'."

"Didn't anyone ever draw a picture of Cleopatra?" the stationmaster wanted to know.

"I don't know. I don't think so."

"Then how the hell do we know if she was even pretty at all, let alone prettier than Lillie Langtry? No, sir, I'm tellin' you that Miss Langtry is the prettiest woman that ever lived, and I'm stickin' by that claim," the stationmaster said. He turned his attention to Gid. "What can I do for you, mister?"

"What time's the next train for Sulphur Springs?"

"Tomorrow mornin', at six o'clock."

"Nothing before then? Not even a freight?"

"Well, there's a freight leavin' at nine tonight. It'll get into Sulphur Springs at midnight. It won't be fittin' to ride on, though. No passenger cars attached."

"I'll ride in a stock car with my horse."

"You'll have to pay for your horse and yourself."

"That's all right," Gid said. "I want to get there tonight."

199

Gid was asleep in the hay when the train stopped at the Sulphur Springs station at a little after midnight. He thanked the freight handler for putting up the ramp that allowed him to lead his horse off the car, then he took the horse back to the livery where he had been keeping him.

Most of the town was quiet, though there was still some activity down at the Bon-Ton. The Saddle Rock, however, was as dark as the general store, the apothecary, the bank, and all the other businesses in town.

Gid moved through the shadows until he reached the Saddle Rock. The doors were locked, but he still had a key to the back door, and he used the key to let himself in. Once inside, he went upstairs and knocked lightly on the door to Lily's room.

The door opened, and Lily peeked through the crack.

"Gid!" she said.

"Shh!" Gid cautioned.

Lily opened the door and Gid stepped inside.

"What are –"

"We'll talk later," Gid said.

He put his hand on her chin, then lifted her head up so he could kiss her. He didn't know if under the circumstances, she would welcome him, but the urgency of her response put his doubts to rest.

"I didn't think I'd ever see you again," she said. "I didn't think you would ever come back."

"I didn't think so either," Gid admitted.

"Why did you?"

"I don't know. It just seemed the right thing to do."

"I'm glad you're back," Lily said.

Chapter Sixteen

"Gid! Gid, wake up!" Lily said, shaking Gid insistently the next morning.

Gid sat up in bed, then reached for his gun. "What is it?" he asked.

"No, there's no danger," Lily said quickly. "It's just that I told Phoebe you were here. She wants to talk to you. She says it's very important."

Gid swung his legs over the edge of the bed, then sat there, naked, as he stretched. "All right," he said. "Send her in."

Lily shook her head. "No, I don't think so," she said with a little smile.

"What do you mean, no?"

"Don't you think it would be better if you put on some clothes?"

Gid chuckled, then reached for his trousers. "All right,"

he said. "I'll put my pants on…then you can send her in."

When Phoebe came into the room a moment later, she had a smile that stretched almost from ear to ear. "Gid, am I glad to see you," she said. "And when you hear what I have to say, you're going to be even more glad to see me."

"Damned if you don't look like the cat that got the bird," Gid said.

"Come down to my room with me, Gid. I have something I want to show you."

Gid looked puzzled. "What is it?"

"Don't ask questions, just come with me. You'll see," Phoebe said mysteriously.

Pulling on his boots, Gid followed Phoebe down the hall to her room. He waited as she opened the door then when she stepped back and invited him in with a sweep of her arm, he stepped inside.

"Hello, Little Brother," Will said.

"Will! You're alive!"

Will chuckled. "Yes. At least, that's what they tell me."

"But I thought…" Gid stammered.

"That's what Doc wanted people to think," Will said.

"I tried to get to you in time to let you know the truth," Phoebe said. "But you were already gone."

"Yeah," Gid said. "Well, I had a little business to take care of, then I thought it might be wise to leave town."

"I heard about the business you took care of," Will

said. "Now, let me ask you a question. What are you doing back in town?"

"The truth? I figured I wasn't going to let Greenwall make me run. It seemed like I was, somehow, turning my back on you. I don't know how to explain it, but that's what it seemed like to me."

"Whatever it is that brought you back, I'm glad to see you here," Will said.

"So, what's our first move?"

"Our first move is to make you the sheriff," Will said.

"What," Gid gasped. He shook his head. "Hell no, there isn't anybody goin' to pin a badge on me."

"We've got to."

"Why do we have to?"

"Because you killed The Albino," Will explained. "If you are a private citizen, Greenwall could perhaps make a case for murder that would stand up, even outside Sulphur Springs. But if you are a sheriff, it could be explained by saying that The Albino was killed when he resisted arrest."

"The son of a bitch didn't resist anything," Gid said. "I just went in there and blew his head off, pure and simple."

Will sighed. "Gid, we're not trying the case here. All we're doing is muddying up the issue a little. This way, you have as much authority as Greenwall. More, if you figure that if it ever actually came to a trial, the town would support you."

"That's true, Gid," Phoebe said.

"But you have to have some justification, and a badge will be that justification."

"Except I won't be legal. The town council that would appoint me isn't even legal."

"Do you think Greenwall's position is legal?"

"No."

"Then your claim to be sheriff would be as legal, and would have as much authority, as Greenwall's claim. A court, an honest court, would have to hear both sides. And I don't really think that Greenwall is ready to take his side to an honest court."

Gid smiled. "I guess you have a point," he said.

"You're damn right I have a point. Phoebe, how about getting our town council called together again?" Will suggested. "I think it's time the town met their new sheriff. And while we're at it, I'll let them know that I'm still alive."

At that same moment, down the street from the Saddle Rock, the door to Ling Lee's laundry opened. Lee, who was hard at work, didn't bother to look up from his ironing board.

"You have laundry for me to do, leave in basket," he called. "You have laundry pickup, I be with you in one minute."

"It ain't laundry we're here for, you yella-skinned bastard."

Ling Lee felt a quick surge of fear bolt through him as he saw Deputies Carnahan and Cutter stepping through the front door.

"What you want?" Ling Lee asked.

Carnahan shut the front door and locked it, then he pulled down the shade and turned the OPEN--CLOSED sign around, to indicate that the laundry was closed.

"What you do? No can close now," Ling Lee said. "Have people who need laundry."

"Oh, yeah, you can close now, Chinaman. And you're going to stay closed until you pay what you owe."

"I owe nothing."

"You owe the sheriff his tax."

Ling Lee shook his head. "No. We have meeting, we take vote, we say, 'no more do we pay sheriff tax.' "

"We know all about that meeting," Cutter said. "But the Crockett boys were there for that meeting, weren't they? They were the ones who gave you the guts to say that. Well, I have news for you, Chinaman. The Crock-etts are gone now, both of 'em. One's dead, and the other hightailed it out of here after committing murder. I don't think you can count on them for help anymore."

"Not count on them," Ling Lee said. "Count on each other."

"Is that a fact? Now, let me see how this works. The idea is that, if nobody pays, then none of you will have to, right?"

"Yes."

"Wrong," Cutter said. "Anyone who doesn't pay will answer to us. And, Chinaman, right now that's you. Are you going to pay the sheriff his rightful taxes, or not?"

"I not pay," Ling Lee said resolutely.

"You think the others will come help you?" Carnahan asked. He laughed. "Nobody is goin' to turn their hand to help a Chinaman. So, you might as well pay."

"I not pay," Ling Lee said again.

"Then I guess we're just going to have to make an example of you," Cutter said. "We need to show the others in this town what will happen to them if they're as dumb as you are."

Gid, Watson, Phoebe, Harry, Levy, and Caswell were sitting around a table at the Saddle Rock. By a special act, "Mayor" Watson had just appointed Gid as the "Provisional Sheriff" of Sulphur Springs.

"What does provisional mean?" Gid asked as he pinned the star onto his shirt.

"It means that you are the sheriff, provided we can get our claim recognized in the capital. If we can, you will be the sheriff in fact."

Gid chuckled. "Well I've never been any kind of a sheriff, provisional or otherwise." He polished the star with the back of his hand, then looked across the table at the others. "How does it look?" he asked.

"I think it fits you, Gid," Harry said. "If you ask me, you were born to be a sheriff."

"That right?" Gid pulled his shirt out and looked at the star. He laughed again. "I'll tell you this. There are more than just a few folks back in Missouri who would be very surprised to hear that."

"So," Watson asked, "how are we doing with the tax repeal? Has anyone encountered any kind of trouble with Greenwall or any of his deputies?"

"So far, so good," Caswell said. "I haven't taken any tax money over to Greenwall's office, and I haven't heard from him."

Levy pulled a cigar from his inner jacket pocket, bit the end from it, then bent down to light it over the lantern that sat in the middle of the table. He took several puffs before he commented.

"I haven't heard anything from him either, but I don't expect Greenwall to roll over and play dead," he said. "I figure he's still trying to come up with some way to handle it. He had too good of a deal going here, and he isn't just going to walk away from it. I believe he's going to try something."

"Let him try," Harry said. "We're ready for him. Especially now that we have our own sheriff."

Suddenly they heard someone shouting outside, and then the rapid footfalls of someone running down the board sidewalk.

"They hung him! They hung him!" someone was shouting outside. "The sheriff and his deputies hung Ling Lee!"

"What?" Harry said. He started toward the door with the others just behind him, then he yelled at the messenger. "What are you saying?"

"The sheriff and his deputies!" the man called back. "They went into Ling Lee's laundry and hauled him out, then carried him down to the hangin' tree. He's down there right now!"

Gid was the first one outside, and he ran down the full length of the street until he came to the hanging tree. There hanging from the outstretched limb, was Ling Lee. His wife and child were standing nearby looking up at him, and though they weren't crying aloud, Gid didn't think he had ever seen faces with more pain.

"Son of a bitch!" Caswell swore, arriving then. "The bastard did do it!"

"Oh, Harry!" Phoebe gasped. She turned away from the twisted neck and grimacing features of the Chinese man who had been a part of the town for as long as

Phoebe had been here.

Attached to Ling Lee's shoe was a sign.

Ling Lee
Nothing is as sure as death and taxes.
Ling Lee give up on the taxes. So now
he is dead.

Chapter Seventeen

As Verndam cut Ling Lee's body down, Greenwall climbed up onto the back of the buckboard to address the people who had been drawn to the scene.

"I want you folks to take a good look over there," he said, pointing toward the front of the jail. In addition to Carnahan, Cutter, and Hooper, who were the only three remaining from Greenwall's original force of deputies, there were three more dangerous-looking men.

"Who are those men?" Watson asked.

"They are my new deputies. As you have said in your newspaper, my force has been cut down somethin' considerable from what it was when I started. So, I sent for some more good men. Three of them arrived this mornin', another three will be here by noon today."

"Greenwall, you have no authority to hire any more deputies. In fact, you no longer have any authority of any kind, because as the new mayor of this town, I am hereby publicly dismissing you," Watson said.

Greenwall looked at Watson with a strange expression on his face.

"I beg your pardon? As the new mayor? What are you talkin' about?"

"You may not be aware of it, but the citizens of this town have reorganized and constituted a new city government. We have a new city council and a new mayor. And as the new mayor, I am now telling you that your services are no longer needed."

Several of the townspeople who were gathered around the hanging tree were now hearing, for the first time, of the action of the merchants' meetings. They made their approval known by applauding.

Greenwall pulled his pistol and fired two shots into the air.

"Hold it! Everyone be quiet!" he shouted. As he was shouting, he was also signaling for his deputies to come up beside him. They responded quickly to Greenwall's call and gathered in a semicircle around him, with pistols drawn. They glared menacingly at the crowd.

"Now, hear these words," Greenwall said. "I'm going to give you merchants until nine o'clock tomorrow mornin' to bring me all the money that you owe. That means all the taxes you have held back, plus a fine."

"A fine?" someone asked.

"Yes, a fine, equal to the amount of tax that you already owe me. That means, by nine tomorrow mornin', you'll have to pay double. Have the money ready, or you'll wind up like the Chinaman, hangin' from this tree."

"You can't hang all of us!" someone shouted from the back of the crowd.

"That may be," Greenwall agreed. "But I figure that won't make much difference to the ones we do hang. Now, you people go on back to your stores and shops and start doin' some business." He chortled mockingly. "After all, if you're gonna pay me tomorrow, you're gonna have to make some money."

Once again, the room at the back of the Saddle Rock was utilized as a meeting place for the new town council. As the various council members arrived for the meeting, their faces reflected obvious signs of worry over the latest turn of events. Even the most nervous, however, agreed that the point of no return had been reached.

"We've come this far," Levy said. "We can't turn back now. Something has to be done."

"I agree with you, Levy," Young said. "But it might be a good idea to pay the taxes tomorrow anyway."

"What? Now, why would you say a damn fool thing like that?" Caswell asked.

"To buy us a little time," Young replied. "Just until we figure out what to do."

"Young might be right," Watkins suggested. "I mean about buying time. At least, until we come up with a plan."

"We've got a plan," Will said, suddenly appearing in the doorway.

"My God!"

"Where did you –?"

"It can't be!"

In addition to the exclamations of surprise, there was a collective gasp from all present, for until this very moment everyone except Gid, Phoebe, Doc Tanner, and Casper Verndam had thought that Will was dead.

Gid was with his brother and wearing a badge. This too was a surprise to most of those present.

"Someone want to explain what's going on here?" Young asked. He looked at Will. "You aren't a ghost, are you?"

"I'm not a ghost," Will answered.

Doc Tanner stood up. "Hugh is right, somebody should explain what's going on, and I reckon that someone is me. I lied when I said that Will Crockett was dead. I lied, and Mr. Verndam backed me up. I needed the time to attend his wounds, and I figured the only way I would get it would be for everyone – especially Greenwall and his deputies – to believe that he really was dead."

"Well, by God, I for one am glad you aren't dead!" Levy said, and his sentiment was seconded by several others.

"Will, you said you have a plan?" Watson asked, trying to get the meeting back on track.

"Yes," Will replied. "I believe that I do. However, it will take the cooperation of the entire town. Everyone must be involved... everyone must do their part."

"You can count on us, Mr. Crockett," Watkins said.

"Yes, you can count on us," several others stated as well.

"Put the plan into operation, Will," Watson said. "You'll have all the cooperation you need."

"Good, good," Will said. He handed a piece of paper to Watson. "I'd like you to print this in your newspaper today."

Watson looked at the paper, then read aloud: "Fifty thousand dollars in new greenbacks to be transferred from the Citizens Bank in Walcox to the First Bank of Pantano. Specie is to be transferred by courier on the seventeenth, instant."

"Put that right in the middle of the first page," Will said. He smiled. "When Greenwall sees that, he's going to go there like flies to honey."

"That'll get the son of a bitch out of town!" Caswell said. Then quickly he apologized to the ladies for his language.

"It will get him out of town," Watson said. "But I don't know if I want to print that."

"Why not?"

"Yes, we would get Greenwall out of our hair...but what about the poor courier who is transporting the money?" Watson shook his head and attempted to hand the note back. "I'm sorry, Mr. Crockett, I wouldn't want it on my conscience if anything happened to the courier."

Will chuckled. "In the first place, there won't be a courier, because there isn't really any money," Will said. "And in the second place, the only one who might be put in danger would be me, because the most logical place to intercept a courier would be at Crowley Ridge. And that's where I intend to be."

"In other words, you're setting yourself up for bait?" Watson asked.

"If you want to catch a fox, you have to bait the trap," Will replied.

"Are you sure you're up for it?" Caswell asked. "I mean, you might not be dead, but you do have a hole in your chest."

"It's a little sore," Will admitted. "But Doc tells me that the danger of havin' the wound mortify on me has passed. I can handle it."

"All right, so we get Greenwall out of town. Then what?"

"I'll take care of Greenwall," Will said.

"You can't handle Greenwall and all his deputies alone. You'll need someone to go with you."

"No, I don't think so. I suspect Greenwall will either be alone, or if anything, no more than one of his deputies will be with him when he shows up. You see, that's a lot of money, and I don't think he will be inclined to split it any more than two ways. That's goin' to leave a few deputies in town."

"And taking care of the deputies who are left behind will be our job," Gid said, standing up, speaking for the first time since the meeting started.

"Our job? You mean you will be here with us?"

"I'm your sheriff, aren't I?" Gid said. Although his question was rhetorical, it received more than a dozen affirmative replies.

"Once we get rid of Greenwall and his deputies," Gid continued, "we'll take over the jailhouse and install our new government."

"I'll be damned!" Caswell said.

"What is it?"

"This really is going to be a revolution, isn't it? I mean a full-scale, all-out, military revolution.

"Carnahan," Greenwall said that afternoon, as he read the paper. "Have you seen this?" He handed the paper over to the man who was now his chief of deputies.

"What is it? A story about how mean we are for hangin' the Chinaman?" Carnahan asked with a laugh.

"That's not the story I'm interested in," Greenwall said. He pointed to the page. "This is the one I'm interested in."

Carnahan glanced at it, then, perking up at the numbers, read the entire article.

"There's a courier transporting fifty thousand dollars?" he said. He whistled softly. "I didn't know there was that much money in the world."

"It's a lot of money, all right," Greenwall agreed. "Too much to let pass by."

"Are you thinkin' on takin' it?" Carnahan asked.

"Hell yes, I'm goin' to take it. I didn't show you this just to be makin' conversation," Greenwall replied.

"Fifty thousand dollars," Carnahan said. "Wait 'til I tell the boys."

Greenwall shook his head. "We ain't goin' to tell the others nothin'," he said.

"Why not? I thought you said we were gonna take it."

"We are." Greenwall smiled. "But I don't plan on splittin' it more'n two ways."

"You talkin' 'bout just the two of us doin' it?"

"Why not? There's two of us, and only one courier," Greenwall said. "That breaks down to twenty-five thousand dollars for each of us."

Carnahan whistled softly. "I wonder how much money it takes for a man to be rich?"

"I don't know," Greenwall answered. "But I can tell you

this. Five minutes with that courier, and we're gonna be a hell of a lot closer to rich than we are now."

"Tomorrow's when we're supposed to collect the tax. What if we ain't back in time?"

"We ain't comin' back."

"We ain't?"

"Think about it," Greenwall said. "With all the money we'll have, we can go anywhere we want and forget about this place. Who needs a couple hundred dollars tax money?"

"Yeah, you're right."

"If Cutter and the others are smart enough to collect it without us…they can have it," Greenwall said.

Because his hardware store was right across the street from the sheriff's office, and from the Bon-Ton saloon, Cliff Caswell was detailed to see whether or not Greenwall had taken the bait that had been planted in the newspaper. The next morning, he saw Greenwall and Carnahan ride out just before six A.M., headed in the direction of Crowley Ridge. He knew then that their plan was working.

He hurried down to the Saddle Rock to give Gid the news.

"All right," Gid said. "This is what we've been waiting for." Gid looked over at Phoebe. "Phoebe, you know any of the girls who work at the Bon-Ton?"

"Yes, I know all of them."

"All right, find some way to get 'em all out of the saloon this morning. When the ball opens, I don't want any of 'em getting hurt."

"I'll get them out."

"Why don't you let me do it?" Lily asked.

Phoebe had not heard Lily come down the stairs. "Lily, what are you doing up so early?" she asked.

"I thought I might be able to help in some way, and this is how I can. I should be the one who gets the girls out. Everyone knows you're part of the council. But I'm just an employee here. It wouldn't be that unusual for you to fire me. That would give me a way to go into the Bon-Ton without arousing suspicion."

"She's right, Phoebe," Caswell agreed.

Phoebe nodded. "All right, Lily. You get the girls out of there. But be careful."

"I will be."

"Now," Gid said, "our next job is to make sure that all the deputies are in the saloon by eight o'clock. Anybody have any ideas how we can do that?"

"What if we make a sign and post it that says, 'All deputies meet in saloon at eight o'clock'?" Harry suggested.

Watkins laughed. "It would be nice if it was that simple."

"Yeah," Levy said, laughing as well.

"No, wait a minute," Kidder said. "I think it might work at that. I mean, most of the deputies are so new they probably won't even question it."

"He may be right, Gid," Watson said. "Assuming the stupid bastards can read."

"All right, we'll try it," Gid agreed. "Who are we going to get to put the sign up? If one of us does it, and he's seen doing it, they'll know something's wrong."

"What if we got one of the girls from the Bon-Ton to do it?" Lily suggested. "She could say Greenwall gave her the sign."

Gid ran his hand through his hair as he thought about the suggestion. "I wish Will was here," he said. "He's a lot smarter at this kind of thing than I am. He'd know what to do."

"Gid, we have to get the deputies in there by eight," Harry said. "I think Lily's suggestion about using one of the girls from the Bon-Ton makes sense. At any rate, time's getting away from us and that's the best we can do for now."

Finally, Gid nodded. "All right. When you get the girls out of there, pick one of them to put up the sign for us."

"What about the customers who might go into the Bon-Ton this morning?" Phoebe said.

"What about them?"

"Well, not all of them are bad people," Phoebe explained. "Some of them are also our customers. Is there some way we can warn them, without letting the deputies know what's going on?"

Suddenly Gid snapped his fingers. "I know," he said. "When we make up that sign, have it say that, due to a meeting of all his deputies, the saloon will be closed to the public today."

"Damn good idea," Harry said. "I sure don't know why they call you the dumb one."

"What?" Gid asked. Then, when he realized that his friend was teasing, he laughed out loud.

"All right," Watson said. "We've all got jobs to do. Let's get them done."

Chapter Eighteen

It was seven o'clock in the morning, and Deputy Cutter was still asleep in his room at the Bon-Ton when one of the girls knocked on his door and began calling quietly for Lizzie Mae, the girl who had spent the night in Cutter's bed. Lizzie Mae was now lying beside him, snoring softly. Though she was the one being called, Cutter was the one who was awakened.

"What is it?" he called irritably. "Who's out there?"

"It's me, Deputy Cutter. Lily Bird."

"Lily Bird? Thought you were workin' at the Saddle Rock."

"I was, but I quit. I want to work down here now."

"Yeah? Will you be here tonight?"

"I hope to be," Lily answered.

Cutter had never been with Lily Bird, but the thought of spending the night with her filled him with a pleasant anticipation.

"Deputy Cutter, is Lizzie Mae with you?"

"What? Yeah, she's with me. Why?"

"I need to see her. It's important. Would you send her out, please?"

"Yeah, you can have her," Cutter grumbled. He pushed on Lizzie Mae's shoulder.

"Get up!" Cutter said roughly.

Lizzie Mae woke up. "What is it?" she asked groggily. "What do you want?"

"I don't want a damn thing," Cutter replied. "But someone out in the hall wants you."

"What do they want me for?"

"How the hell do I know? Get up and go out there and see."

"Uhmm, and I was sleepin' so good too."

"You was snorin' like a hog," Cutter growled. "Now get on out there and see what she wants. That way, maybe I can get a little rest."

"Do you want me to come back, honey?"

"No, I don't want you to come back, honey," Cutter said, mimicking her voice. Cutter didn't mind having a woman spend the night with him, but come morning, he would just as soon they be gone. As far as he was concerned, Lily Bird's knock on the door was a fortuitous event.

Lizzie Mae slipped into her clothes quickly, then

stepped out of the room. Cutter heard them whispering outside, and he put the pillow over his head to block them out. Whatever they had to say couldn't possibly be important enough to interrupt his sleep.

Cutter did manage to go back to sleep, though it didn't last long. A short while later there was another loud, impatient knocking on the door, followed by a man's gruff voice.

"Cutter! Cutter, you asleep?"

"Who the hell can sleep with all this bangin' and yellin'?" Cutter replied irritably.

Cutter got out of bed and walked over to the door. When he jerked it open, he saw Deputy Hooper standing there.

"Dammit all to hell, Hooper, what's goin' on around here this mornin'?" Cutter asked. "First that damn woman wakes me up, and now you. What do you want?"

"Greenwall has called a meeting for ever'body at eight-thirty. It's pert' near that now."

"A meetin'? What for? We don't need no meetin'. If the people don't pay their taxes, we know what to do."

"I don't know what it's about," Hooper said. "But it must be important. I've never knowed him to call no meetin' before. He wants ever'one to be downstairs."

Cutter ran a hand through his tousled hair, then scratched his chin. "All right," he said. "All right, tell 'im to hold his horses. I'll be down in a few minutes."

Cutter poured some water from the pitcher into the basin and splashed some of it onto his face. Then he got dressed, pulled on his boots, and strapped on his gun.

As Cutter reached for his hat, he happened to look out through the window. He saw Levy and Kidder going into the still-closed hardware store. Seeing two of the local businessmen going into a closed store wasn't, in itself, all that strange. But both were carrying rifles, and that was curious.

He didn't give it that much thought, though, as he finished dressing then went downstairs. There, he saw all the deputies sitting around the tables, talking quietly among themselves. Only Hooper was there from the original deputies. The other six were men that Greenwall had only recently hired.

The new men sat apart from Hooper. Carnahan, Cutter, and Hooper had not accepted the new deputies with open arms. As far as they were concerned, the new men weren't needed, and their presence just meant there would be more pieces cut from the pie. Pieces that would have otherwise gone to them.

As Cutter thought of Carnahan, he realized that he wasn't there. Neither was Greenwall.

"So, where is he?" Cutter asked as he came over to the table where Hooper was sitting alone.

"Greenwall, or Carnahan?" Hooper replied.

"Either one of 'em. Where are they?"

"Don't know," Hooper answered. "Haven't seen either one of 'em this morning."

"What do you mean, you haven't seen either one of 'em? How the hell did you know we were supposed to have a meetin' if you ain't seen either one of 'em?"

"'Cause of the sign that's posted on the door over there," Hooper said.

"Sign on the door?"

Cutter went over to look at the sign Hooper had told him about.

Notice: I want all deputies to meet in the saloon at 8:30. The saloon will be closed then, and all others must leave. By order of Sidney Greenwall, Sheriff.

"Ain't never know'd Greenwall to leave no sign before," Cutter said. He rubbed his chin, then looked at the group of new deputies. "Any of you see Greenwall this mornin'?" he asked.

All shook their heads no.

"What is it, Cutter?" Hooper asked, seeing that Cutter was beginning to wonder about things.

"I don't know," Cutter replied. "Somethin' just don't seem right about this, is all. Greenwall calls this meetin', but he ain't here. There is somethin'..." Cutter started to say, but as he couldn't put his finger on what was bothering him, he was unable to form the words to express his concern. As a result, he let the incomplete sentence dangle in the air, teasing with its potential.

"What is it, Cutter?" Hooper asked. Totally unaware of anything unusual going on.

"Ah, probably nothin'," Cutter finally said. "I need a drink."

"Kind of early in the mornin' for that, ain't it, Cutter?" One of the new deputies asked.

Angrily, Cutter whirled toward the deputy who had made the comment. He pointed at him. "By damn, if I say I need a drink, who the hell are you to question it?" Cutter asked angrily.

"Didn't mean nothin' by it," the new deputy replied, throwing his hands up as if to ward Cutter off. "I was just passin' a remark, that's all."

"You pass your damn remarks to someone else," Cutter growled. He walked around behind the bar and poured his own liquor, standing there for a moment while he tossed the drink down.

When he finished the drink, he slapped the shot glass down on the bar. "All right," he said. "So, what the hell is goin' on here? What's this meeting about, and why ain't Greenwall here?"

"Ain't nobody figured that out yet," one of the new

deputies said.

"Anybody think to knock on his bedroom door?"

"I already did," Hooper replied. "I checked his room and I checked Carnahan's room. Ain't neither one of 'em here."

"What do you mean they ain't here?"

"Hell, I don't know no other way to tell it, other 'n to say there ain't neither one of 'em there."

Cutter walked over to the batwing doors and looked out onto the street. To his surprise, he didn't see anyone: not one wagon, horse, or pedestrian. He looked toward Caswell's Hardware Store but saw nothing there either.

"What day is this?" he asked.

"I don't know. September something or the other."

"No, I mean what day of the week? Is this Sunday?"

"No. It's Thursday, I think. Or maybe Friday."

"You sure it ain't Sunday?"

"I'm positive it ain't Sunday. Why do you ask?"

"I don't know," Cutter replied. "It just seems awful quiet for some reason. I mean, have you looked out into the street? There ain't nobody or nothin' out there."

"Wonder where Greenwall is," Hooper said.

"Go wake up the girls," Cutter ordered. "Maybe one of 'em will know where they are."

"Ain't none of the girls here," one of the new deputies answered.

"What do you mean?"

"I seen 'em all leavin' here, 'bout forty-five minutes ago."

"You saw the girls leavin'? All of 'em? Where was they goin'?"

"I don't know, but they seemed dammed determined to get out of here. I figured they just didn't want to be here durin' the meetin'."

Cutter looked over at Hooper. "Look here, Hooper, there's somethin' wrong here. Take a look outside."

"Take a look at what?" Hooper replied. "You said yourself there wasn't nothin' out there."

"Take a look," Cutter said again. "Tell me if you see anyone."

Hooper walked over to the door to look outside. "Just them fellas fixin' the roof up on top of the hardware store."

"Some folks fixin' a roof? Where?"

Hooper pointed across the street. "Up there, on the roof of the hardware store. Patchin' it, I guess. Oh, and there's somebody on the roof of the feed store too. What the hell is this, fix your roof day or somethin'?"

Cutter moved quickly to the door and looked up toward the roof. He saw someone running, bent over at the waist.

"Fixin' a roof, my ass. That son of a bitch is carrying a rifle!" Cutter said.

Now it all came together for him.

230

"Get your guns out, men, we're about to be attacked!"

"What are you talkin' about, attacked," one of the new deputies asked. "Who's attackin' us? Injuns?" He laughed at his joke.

"No, damn it! The town is!" Cutter shouted back. "Hell, half the damn town is crawlin' around out there on roofs and behind buildings. And they've all got rifles."

At the same time, Hooper saw someone with a rifle looking out of one of the upstairs rooms at the hotel.

"Son of a bitch! Cutter's right!" Hooper shouted. He drew his pistol and shot toward the hotel. His bullet punched a hole in the glass window, but other than that, it did no damage.

"What did you shoot for, you dumb bastard?" Cutter shouted.

"What do you mean, why did I shoot? I seen someone at the hotel pointin' a rifle this way."

"As long as they thought they had us in the dark, we had the advantage," Cutter said. "Now they know we know."

"So what? There ain't nothin' out there but a bunch of ribbon clerks and store keeps," Hooper said derisively.

"Yeah? Well a lot of ribbon clerks 'n store keeps fought 'n the war, 'n there was a hell of lot killin' that went on," Cutter said.

"Yeah, well if you ask me, I think we ought to just

go out there and –unnnh!"

Hooper's declaration was cut short by a bullet fired from somewhere across the street. The bullet caught him high in the chest and spun him around. He went down, spewing a little fountain of blood. He looked up with the expiration of surprise on his face.

"A ribbon clerk," he said. "Who would've thought…" Those were his last words.

"Get these tables turned over, men!" Cutter shouted. "Get 'em up to the windows! We've got a fight on our hands!"

Gid was climbing onto the roof of the hardware store when he heard the shooting start. He was carrying a heavy box and his movement was somewhat restricted. He set the box down and looked around as the other men on the roof, all of whom were armed with rifles, were firing into the saloon across the street.

"What did you start shooting for? he asked. "I thought we were going to wait for the signal."

"We couldn't help it, Gid," Harry replied. "They must've seen us, 'cause they started the shootin'."

"All right, it doesn't matter," Gid said. He opened the box to reveal several small, hastily made bombs, consisting of empty bean cans filled with blasting powder. Gid picked one of them up.

"All right," he said. "Harry, light the fuse, then step back. I'll throw it."

"Right," Harry said. Harry lit the fuse, and when it was sputtering, Gid stood up and threw it across the street, towards the Bon-Ton. It crashed through one of the windows on the other side.

Gid got down to wait for the blast. He was surprised when, a second later, the bomb, still unexploded, came back out of the saloon. It went off with a roar, in the middle of the street.

"Damn!" Gid said. "I gave them too much time. The fuse was too long."

Gid cut the fuse on the next bomb half as long as the first one. "Now light it," he said. "We'll try it again."

"Gid, that's much too short. It'll go off in your hand."

"No, it won't. Light it," Gid insisted.

Harry lit the fuse and Gid stood up to throw it. This time the bomb exploded in midair, halfway between the roof of the hardware store and the saloon. The fuse was indeed too short.

"All right," Gid said, picking up another one. "This time we'll get it right."

Once more Gid cut the fuse, though not quite as short as he had cut the previous one. Again, the fuse was lit, and again Gid stood up to throw it. The defenders in the saloon concentrated their fire on Gid. Bullets hit the false front wall of the hardware store just in front of him and whizzed by his ear as they burned the air close to him. None of the bullets found their mark, however, and Gid was able to throw yet a third bomb.

A little stream of smoke marked the path of the missile as it hurtled from the top of the hardware store, across the street, then down toward the front window of the Bon-Ton. It broke out some more of the window as it went inside.

This time the fuse was perfectly cut, for an instant after the bomb broke through the window, there was a deafening blast from within the saloon. Fire, smoke, glass shards from the windows, and splinters of the batwing doors blew out into the street.

Four deputies came outside then, firing as they ran, pointing their pistols at the buildings of the town and shooting randomly. To a man, they were cut down by a hail of gunfire from the citizen militia that had been raised for the occasion.

"Cease fire!" Gid shouted, holding his hand up to get attention. "Cease fire!"

The firing stopped and for a moment there was absolute silence. Then, when the citizens of the town realized that they had won their revolution, they began to cheer.

Doc Tanner was the first one to go down onto the street. There, he began examining the bodies to see if anyone was left alive. The others joined him in the street, laughing and talking about their victory, happy and proud that once again the town belonged to them.

Phoebe, Lily, Helga, and the other women, as well as the children of the town, had taken shelter in the basement of the hardware store. Now the three women ventured out into the street with the men to see what was going on.

"I'd better check inside," Doc said. "There may be some wounded in there."

"If there are, you may need some help," Lily said. "I'll go with you."

"Thanks," Doc said.

Shortly after they went inside, there was a muffled shot. Startled, Gid and the others looked toward the bomb-damaged front of the saloon. A moment later, they could see Doc coming through the wreckage. He had a strange expression on his face, and it took only a moment to see why.

Doc was walking at the point of a gun. He was being held hostage.

"All right!" Cutter said, waving his pistol around. He had the advantage over the citizens of the town, not only because he was holding Doc Tanner hostage, but also because he had a loaded pistol, whereas the small citizens' army had been equipped with rifles, most of which were now left behind them.

"I want a horse!" Cutter shouted. "I want a horse, and I want five hundred dollars in greenbacks! If I don't have it in one minute, Doc dies."

"You realize, don't you, that if you kill him, you won't have any hold over us?" Gid cautioned him.

"I don't give a damn!" Cutter shouted. "Do you understand me? I don't give a damn. I already killed the whore who came in with him, for setting us up this morning. If I kill one more of you bastards before you kill me, I can die a happy man. Now get me a horse and that money." Cutter smiled an evil smile. "You folks been wantin' to get rid of me, here's your chance."

At the news of Lily's death, Gid was ready to leap at the devil, but suddenly the flat, popping sound of a single rifle shot echoed from the adjacent buildings. A bullet hole appeared in Cutter's forehead and he fell back into the street, his head landing in a pile of horse manure.

"What the hell?" Kidder asked. "Who fired that shot?"

"Ja, I fired the shot," Helga said, stepping out through the front door of her café. From the end of the barrel of the rifle she was holding, there arose a small, curling stream of smoke.

"You killed him, Helga?" Gid asked. He smiled. "Well, I didn't know you had it in you, but I'm glad you did."

Helga walked over to the body then stood there, looking down at it. She spit on Cutter's body. "Three months ago, this man raped me," she said.

"This son of a bitch raped you?" Watkins asked, surprised by the announcement. "Why, Helga, you should have told someone."

"And who would I tell?" Helga asked. "The sheriff? Maybe if I tell the sheriff, he might do it too. No, there was no one to help, so I keep my shame to mine own self."

Watkins nodded in agreement. "I reckon you've got a point there," he said.

"I tell him then, that someday I will kill him. He laugh at me then," Helga said. She stared for a long moment at Cutter's still form. "I do not think he laugh now."

Chapter Nineteen

Will was aware that the two men were following him, riding parallel with him. He also knew that when they left him, they would ride ahead in order to get into position to set up an ambush. The ambush point would be just ahead, where the trail squeezed down to a narrow path going through a needlelike draw at Crowley Ridge. Recalling his days with Quantrill, he knew that at the other end of the draw, a real courier would be a sitting duck.

Will reached the draw, where for the next several seconds he would be out of the line of sight of those who were waiting for him. This was where he would make his move. As he passed under a large rock outcropping, he stood in his saddle, found a good handgrip, then pulled himself up. Once in the rocks, he was able to climb over the top of the pass while his horse continued on through.

Will ran at a crouch to the far end of the pass. From there, he could hear the slow, measured clop of his horse's hooves echoing through the long, narrow canyon. He pulled his pistol and waited…just as he knew that Greenwall and Carnahan were doing.

The sound of the hoofbeats came closer until they were almost upon him.

"Now!" Will heard Greenwall shout, and the narrow chasm was filled with the sound of exploding gunshots and whistling bullets.

Will's riderless horse bolted out of the canyon.

"What the hell? Where is he?" Carnahan asked.

"We must've got 'im! Grab the horse!" Greenwall ordered. "The money will be in the saddlebags!"

Carnahan stepped in front of the horse and threw his arms up. The horse slid to a stop, its iron hooves striking sparks on the rocky ground. Carnahan grabbed the halter and began to calm the horse.

"You hold him," Greenwall said, starting toward the saddlebags. "I'll get the money."

"There isn't any money," Will said, suddenly standing up.

"What the hell? It's Crockett!" Carnahan shouted. "But how can it be? I thought The Albino killed you."

"He did kill me," Will said. "But I've come back from hell to get you."

"What? You're a ghost?"

"He ain't no ghost," Greenwall said. "Ghosts don't need guns. Shoot the son of bitch!"

Greenwall and Carnahan raised their guns to shoot but Will shot twice, the shots coming so close together that it sounded like one sustained roar. When the smoke cleared, both Greenwall and Carnahan had dropped their guns.

"Why didn't you kill us?" Greenwall asked, clamping his left hand over his wounded right hand.

"I've got other plans for you," Will replied.

"Would you answer a question for me?" Greenwall asked. "The whole town turned out for your funeral. If that wasn't you in the box, who was it?"

"It was your friend, The Albino."

Greenwall laughed dryly. "I got to hand it to you, Crockett. That's one of the slickest tricks I ever heard, makin' the whole town think you was dead like that. You put one over on us. Now, I'll be interested to see how you handle it when you get us back to town. You don't really think my deputies are going to let you put me in jail, do you?"

"When they learn that you planned to steal the bank money and leave them high and dry, I think they might."

Greenwall chuckled. "You think they'll believe you? Not for a minute. If you're smart, you'll just ride off now, otherwise, you'll be spendin' the night in jail, 'n come mornin', I'll hang you."

"We'll just see who gets hanged, and who does the hangin'," Will said.

It wasn't yet late afternoon when Will led his two prisoners back into Sulphur Springs. There were people on the street, more people than he had ever seen on the streets before.

"What is this?" Greenwall asked. "What's goin' on? Somethin' seems different."

Will saw at once what was different. The people of Sulphur Springs, who were normally reticent and withdrawn, were now laughing and animated. As he passed the Bon-Ton, he saw why. There, in front of the broken window, not in coffins but tied to boards, were the bodies of eight deputies.

"Greenwall, my God, look over there!" Carnahan shouted in alarm. "They're dead, all of 'em!"

Will looked toward Greenwall and saw the façade of bravado fall away. It wasn't until that very moment that Greenwall realized he was truly the captive and not the captor.

When Will stopped in front of the sheriff's office, he was met by his brother and several of the town's citizens.

"Well, Little Brother, looks like your plan worked,"

Will said as he swung down from the saddle.

"I'll say it did," Watkins replied. He saw the sullen, unarmed, Greenwall and Carnahan. "And with them two, we can make a clean sweep of it."

"So, what are we going to do with 'em?" Kidder asked.

"What do you mean, what are we goin' to do?" Watkins replied. "We're goin' to hang 'em."

"We can't do that," Kidder said.

"Why not?"

"It wouldn't be legal. I mean, we took our town from these people in the first place because of their lawlessness. I don't want us to become just as lawless, 'n hangin' 'em without a trial would be nothing more than a lynching."

"Well, hell, we'll give the bastards a trial, then hang 'em," Watkins suggested.

"We don't have a judge here. How are we going to do that?"

"Wait a minute, George," Watson said. "You know, we do have some precedence here. I think we could hang them and make it legal."

"How?"

"We had a revolution, right? An armed revolution?"

"Yes."

"That puts us under martial law. And, as we are subject to martial law, we, the Sulphur Springs militia, can convene a court, select a jury, and appoint a prosecutor and counselor for the defense."

Greenwall's face went gray. "You can't do that," he said. "You got no right to do that."

"What are you bitching about, Greenwall? At least you are going to get a trial. That's more of a chance then you ever gave anyone else," Will said.

"Whatever you do here won't stand up in a real court, and you know it!" Greenwall said.

"I am the mayor now," Watson said. "I will take it upon myself to convene the court. If there are any questions with the legitimate authorities later on, I will be solely responsible for my actions, and I will take my case all the way to the Supreme Court, if necessary."

"You're saying you would take this case to the Supreme Court?" Greenwall asked.

"I'll take it there if I have to," Watson said with a cold smile. "But trust me, it won't matter to the two of you. You'll both be long dead by then."

Though the trial began less than an hour later, the entire town had gotten word of it so that nearly everyone was squeezed into the empty Bon-Ton saloon to watch. The fact that eight bodies had not been removed and were still standing their ghostly watch added a touch of the macabre to the proceedings. In addition, they could see the bomb damage as half the bar had been blown away, the shelf had been cleared of the whiskey bottles, and the mirror knocked down from its position behind the bar.

Caswell had been appointed prosecutor, and he opened the argument by charging Greenwall with terrorizing a town and murdering the four cowboys by their mock trial and illegal hanging. He chose that incident, rather than the hanging of Ling Lee, because no one actually saw Ling Lee until after he was already hanged. On the other hand, almost the entire town was present for the hanging of the four cowboys.

Caswell interviewed several witnesses, all of whom told how they had watched while the young cowboys were placed on the back of a buckboard wagon with ropes around their necks, and how the buckboard team was caused to dash forward, jerking the buckboard from under the young cowboys' feet, causing them to be hanged. Telling the details of the hanging to the judge and jury was an exercise in redundancy since the judge and every member of the jury had also witnessed it.

Harry Connors had been appointed as the defense attorney, and as soon as Caswell sat down, he cross-examined the witnesses.

"Mr. Levy, when the cowboys were hanged, was it by a large, unruly mob?"

"Well, there were a lot of people there."

"Was the crowd unruly? Did its members participate

in the hanging?"

"No. Only the sheriff and his deputies participated."

"Were the sheriff and his deputies wild and unruly?"

Levy looked over at Greenwall. "No," he said. "They were cold and calculating."

"Have you ever been the witness to a legal hanging?" Harry asked.

"Yes. I saw me a hangin' in Tucson."

"A legal hanging?"

"Oh, yes, it was legal, all right."

"How would you describe it? The legal hanging, I mean. Was it wild and unruly? Or cold and calculating?"

"Well, I guess you could call it cold and calculating," Levy replied, realizing that he was using the same words of description.

"Then, in your mind, the only thing that was different about this hanging from the one in Tucson is that you don't believe this one was legal?"

"I know this one wasn't legal."

"But it was prescribed by the court, wasn't it?"

"By Greenwall's court."

"But it was a court, not a mob lynching."

"I suppose you could call it that."

"Thank you. No further questions."

As Greenwall and Carnahan both refused to testify in their own behalf, the court was then over, except for the summation. Harry stood up and faced the jury that had been selected from among the townspeople.

"Gentlemen of the jury, the defendants, Sidney Greenwall and Roy Carnahan, are not the kind of men you would want as neighbors, or friends, and certainly not as your enemy. They are men who have lived for many years by their guns, and there is no doubt in my mind that they have killed many men. But we are not trying them for living by their guns, nor for killing many men. We are bringing them to trial on a very specific charge, and that is the charge of murder, by hanging, of the four young cowboys about whom we have already spoken.

"If that is all we can find to try them on, then I've got some bad news for you. You can't find them guilty. All you have to do is recall the testimony of Mr. Levy to see that it wasn't murder. It was a court-ordered execution.

"But, what court, you may ask. I will answer you. It is the same court we are in now, gentlemen, for according to Mr. Caswell, the prosecutor in this case, the very legality of what we are doing now is based upon the establishment of a court in this town by Sheriff Sidney Greenwall. We cannot find his court illegal for him, and legal for ourselves. We can't have it both ways." Harry looked over at Greenwall and Carnahan, who were now smiling smugly. "These two men are guilty of a lot of things…but they aren't guilty of the charges that have been filed against them today."

The townspeople, who had thought that perhaps Harry Connors would mount a listless defense, now sat stunned by the effectiveness of his argument. Caswell sat at the prosecutor's table for a full moment, marshaling his thoughts, before he stood up and walked over to address the jury.

"Gentlemen of the jury," he said. "Harry Connors has, indeed, given us something to consider. He has said that we cannot find Greenwall's court illegal without finding ourselves illegal for using the same court. And there is merit to his argument, for, in the final analysis, we must be certain that we not only have the legal right to do what we are doing, but also the moral authority.

"The question is, then, can we use this court to try Sidney Greenwall and Roy Carnahan? And if this court finds them guilty and sentences them to death by hanging, can we carry out that terrible sentence without being accomplices to murder, and sustaining permanent damage to our legal status as a civilized community, and to our immortal souls?"

Caswell crossed his arms to study the jury and saw that, to a man, he had their rapt attention.

"The answer to that question is...yes. We can act as a court. Because you see, gentlemen, the court itself is not on trial here. What is on trial here is the perversion of that court, as was perpetrated by these two men. You can find Greenwall and Carnahan guilty of perverting the court to commit the murder of those four young cowboys, while at the same time affirming the legality of the court itself. Therefore, I urge you to return a verdict of guilty."

Clarence Watson, now acting as judge of the court, turned to the jury. "The jury may now retire to deliberate," he said.

While the jury was in deliberation, Will, Gid, Phoebe, Watson, Caswell, and Harry Connors waited.

"I must tell you, Harry, I expected you to roll over. I was quite impressed at the defense you put up for those two men."

"And I am equally impressed by the logic of your prosecution," Harry replied. "Did you study law?"

"I read for it, yes," Caswell replied. "But unless a man lives in a big city with several opportunities to ply his avocation…he could starve."

Harry laughed. "I know," he said. "That's why I'm a bartender."

"Why, Harry Connors," Phoebe said, "you mean you also read for the law?"

"Yes," Harry said.

"My. I am very impressed with my new business partner," she said.

"The jury is comin' back," someone shouted from the rear of the building, and everyone took their seats to await the verdict. When the jury was seated, Watson looked toward Watkins, who had been selected as foreman of the jury.

"Has the jury reached a verdict?" Watson asked.

"We have, Your Honor," Watkins replied, playing out his role with solemnity.

"How find you?"

"To the charge of terrorizing the town, we find the defendants not guilty." Watkins looked out over the townspeople. "We figure we are the guilty ones for lettin' 'em get away with it for so long."

There were several gasps and groans of protest from those in the audience, and Watson, using a carpenter's hammer as a gavel, banged it on the table several times in a call for order.

Greenwall and Carnahan smiled smugly.

"How find you as to the second charge?" Watson asked.

"To the charge of murdering the four young cowboys, we find the defendants guilty."

This time the audience erupted into cheers and applause and, again, Watson had to bang his gavel for quiet. Finally, with the audience silent, Watson cleared his throat.

"Thank you, gentlemen of the jury. You are now dismissed. Will the prisoners please stand?"

Greenwall and Carnahan, their beady eyes now reflecting fear, stood.

"Sidney Greenwall and Roy Carnahan, you have been tried by a court that was established by yourselves, validated by martial law, and presided over by me. This court has found you both guilty of murder in the first degree, and therefore I sentence you both to be hanged by the neck until you are dead. Sentence is to be carried out tomorrow morning. Please escort the prisoners across the street to the jail. This court is adjourned."

As four men stepped up to grab the two prisoners, Greenwall looked over to Will and Gid.

"You two boys come early tomorrow," he said. "You'll get to see us dance."

Will shook his head. "You'll have to do it without us," he said. "We sold our interest in the Saddle Rock, and Gid has turned in his badge. We'll be moving on."

"What? You mean you've sold out? You're leaving town?"

"That's right."

Greenwall looked puzzled. "I don't understand," he said. "If you're leaving town, why were you so all fired up to get me? What was in it for you?"

"Nothing," Will replied.

"Then, why did you do it?"

Will smiled. "Some things you do just for the hell of it," he said.

After Greenwall and Carnahan had been put in jail, Will, Gid, Phoebe and Harry were in the mortician's office, looking at the body of Lily Bird.

"You did a good job, Mr. Luscombe," Phoebe said. "Lily always was a pretty woman, now she isn't only pretty she's ... I feel strange saying this, but there is an innocent look about her."

"She was innocent," Gid said. "Yes, I know she was a prostitute, but that was only her body. She had an innocent soul."

"I wish we knew her real name," Phoebe said. "I would want it to be on her headstone, but she never told me what it was."

"It was Lucy Raster," Gid said.

"She told you?"

"Yes," Gid said.

After Lucy Raster's funeral, Will and Gid were having a goodbye drink with Phoebe and Harry at the Saddle Rock.

"Gid, what do you want to do with this?" Phoebe asked, putting a roll of bills on the table. "I found it in Lily's, I mean Lucy's room when I was looking for a dress to bury her in."

Gid recognized it as the money he had given her.

"I think we should give it to her family," Gid said, as he pushed the money back toward Phoebe.

"What are you doing?" Phoebe asked, confused by his action.

Gid smiled at her. "You are her family."

As Will and Gid rode away, the town of Sulphur Springs grew smaller in the distance behind them. They could have stayed there—now that Greenwall was gone the town had promise. But that would have required putting down roots, and that was something neither brother wanted to do.

A Look At: Panhandle Justice (The Crocketts' Western Saga: Five)

Best-selling author Robert Vaughan shows the human side of the wild west.

There's a reason this town's name is Epitaph...The Crockett brothers stroll into Epitaph, Arizona – and find themselves hip deep in a war. On one side's the ranchers, other side's the miners.

But with the Crocketts in town, every two-bit gunslinger's chances of surviving are just about zero...

AVAILABLE OCTOBER 2021

About the Author

Robert Vaughan sold his first book when he was 19. That was 57 years and nearly 500 books ago. He wrote the novelization for the mini-series Andersonville. Vaughan wrote, produced, and appeared in the History Channel documentary Vietnam Homecoming.

His books have hit the NYT bestseller list seven times. He has won the Spur Award, the PORGIE Award (Best Paperback Original), the Western Fictioneers Lifetime Achievement Award, received the Readwest President's Award for Excellence in Western Fiction, is a member of the American Writers Hall of Fame and is a Pulitzer Prize nominee.

Vaughan is also a retired army officer, helicopter pilot with three tours in Vietnam. And received the Distinguished Flying Cross, the Purple Heart, The Bronze Star with three oak leaf clusters, the Air Medal for valor with 35 oak leaf clusters, the Army Commendation Medal, the Meritorious Service Medal, and the Vietnamese Cross of Gallantry.

Printed in Great Britain
by Amazon

26843645R00148